CANYON
A Novel by
James W. Foster

Copyright © 2005 by Jim Foster

•••

1.

As the sun continued its retreat into the west casting its fading rays upon her corner of the world, the girl stirred awake. Night was falling, and under it's cloak was the safe time for her and her people to carry on with the majority of their daily business.

This was the only way of life the girl had ever known. Darkness was a haven, a friend for her and her people. It was daylight that produced tales of their version of the boogeyman, outsiders. All outsiders were to be feared, and Mala knew that anyone she didn't recognize was an outsider and therefore an enemy.

Under no circumstance was she to allow herself to be seen by an outsider. Great pains were taken by the Sasquatch Indians to keep sightings to a minimum. Strict rules were enforced to ensure that every member of the tribe avoided being sighted by outsiders at all costs. Accidents were forgivable, but if it was deemed that a sighting by an outsider was due to negligence the penalty would be extremely harsh.

Mala was excited. Tonight there was to be a wedding and that meant a distraction. Except for the unmarried females who were afraid of attracting the attention of The Other, the whole tribe would be in attendance, and it was under circumstances such as these that Mala could escape the canyon, and was briefly free to roam.

She knew that leaving the canyon and the tribe's network of caves and tunnels was extremely risky. Not only to herself because of the wicked punishment she knew awaited her if ever she were caught, but to the entire tribe.

1

The Sasquatch Indians had concealed themselves for generations, and The Other, who had led her people into the canyon all those generations ago had warned them that discovery by the outsiders of the world beyond their little haven would be disastrous to them. It would indeed be the end of their way of life, the end of their tribe. This had been drilled into each of their minds from the day they were old enough to comprehend such warnings, and they all feared The Other too much to openly doubt him.

In spite of all of this, Mala was unable to resist the urge to slip away from time to time when the opportunity arose.

2.

Late on a hot Saturday afternoon in late spring, two dark-haired boys walked along a quiet residential street in a little town called Vollmer's Hollow. Each of them carried a fishing pole and small tackle box. On weekends when the weather was warm, these two could often be found with their fishing poles in hand. Summer vacation was still a few weeks away, but already Shawn and Denny Jackson were sporting deep farmer's tans from many hours spent out in the sun.

The young brothers were returning home from yet another day at their favorite fishing spot in front of an unused fishing shanty. The shanty was located on a channel running inland from Lake Sasquatch. Today they had only caught a few small rock bass, but what they caught was only of secondary concern to the boys, it was simply the act of being outside that mattered to them most.

Occasionally the boys did catch something that was worth keeping. Sometimes there were brown and lake trout in the channel, and there was always perch and pickerel to be caught as well as a large variety of other fish.

The favorite of both boys was catfish. Even a smallish catfish put up a pretty good fight, and their father liked to eat the ugly things.

"This is considered a delicacy in the southern states," he had explained to his sons.

Shawn and Denny loved to bring catfish home, or more precisely, they loved to watch their father clean the catfish that they brought home. Mike Jackson had a slick way of cleaning these fish. First he nailed them to a board in the garage. Then he took a sharp knife and severed the

3

fish's backbone, first just under its gills, and then at the tail. After that he took a pair of vise grips, clamped them onto the backbone and pulled. The backbone came away from the head and tail bringing along with it the fillets that would soon find their way to the frying pan. When the senior Jackson was done with this little operation he'd look over at his fascinated sons and wink.

"Hungry?" He'd ask them.

The boys would decline grimacing. They had no inclinations to join their father in the delicacy, they weren't nearly as big on eating fish as they were on catching them. They didn't really like any fish unless it was Captain Highliner, or Hind Liner as Denny liked to call it. Watching their father skin them was reward enough to the boys for bringing a catfish home.

Knowing how much their sons enjoyed the outdoors, Shawn and Denny's parents thought that it might be a good idea to enroll the two into boy scouts. When they asked the boys about it, Shawn, the older and usually more responsible of the two, took to the idea right away, and his enthusiasm alone was all it took for Mike and Patty Jackson to make the decision final.

Denny on the other hand, was a little more reluctant about it than his older brother. He thought that the uniforms looked ridiculous, and that boy scouts was a club for geeks. He would much rather have been signed up for baseball. It didn't matter how he felt about it though, his brother had spoken up so quickly that Denny hadn't been given a chance to voice his opinion on the matter. They were going to be enrolled into scouts and that was that.

"You've got a big mouth," he told Shawn.

4

It was the night of the day that they'd been signed up. Denny and Shawn shared a bedroom and slept in bunk beds. They usually talked for a while each night before they fell to sleep.

"What's that supposed to mean?" Asked Shawn.

"Ya, ya, Mom and Dad, we'd love to be in boy scouts," said Denny, mimicking Shawn in a nasal tone. Then he said, "I don't wanna join no stupid boy scouts."

"Why not?"

"Boy scouts is for turds. Johnny and Lester Sabina are in boy scouts."

Shawn laughed, he hadn't thought of that. Johnny and Lester where the supreme geeks of Vollmer's Hollow Public School. They were identical twins and they clung to each other almost like they were still in the womb. All of the other kids steered clear of Lester and Johnny, at least most of the time. The exception was to get them to eat stuff. For a quarter, the platinum headed twins would eat just about anything. Bugs, rocks, garbage, and things like that. It never failed to amaze the other kids. The 'Trashcan Twins,' as they were called, made all kinds of money just for eating things that grossed everyone out.

There was a drawback to being the one to pay to see this spectacle. Often times after they had earned a quarter from someone, the Trashcan Twins would follow him around for the remainder of the recess. It didn't matter what you said to them, or what names you called them, or how you threatened them, they wouldn't go away. They wouldn't say anything, the Sabina twins rarely ever spoke, they'd just follow whomever had paid the quarter like two silent shadows.

Shawn didn't find the idea of being around the trash can twins to be nearly as much of a deterrent against

5

joining scouts as Denny did, and he continued to try to persuade his younger brother that scouts really could wind up being a lot of fun for them.

"Bobby's in scouts, and Carl too. You like them don't you?"

"Bobby's in scouts?" Denny asked in disbelief. "I didn't know that."

Denny thought quite highly of Bobby. He was in Denny's class. He had flaming red hair and freckles, and it seemed to Denny that the only thing Bobby was interested in was football. He played football every single recess in school, and he knew everything there was to know about the sport. He'd told all of the other boys in his class that he was going to be in the NFL when he grew up, and Denny didn't doubt that one day Bobby would do just that.

Bobby was a tough kid. He wasn't remarkably large, but he was very strong for his age, and he was known throughout the school to possess a bad temper if his buttons were pushed. On more than one occasion Bobby had bloodied the nose of kids a year or two older, and a head taller than himself for making the mistake of trying to bully him or one of his friends. When left alone, Bobby had a cheerful demeanor, and those who knew him knew that he was also very loyal to his friends. A friend of Bobby's could always rest assured that they needn't ever worry about being bullied. Bobby wasn't afraid of anyone, and if he thought that one of his buddies was being treated any other way than they ought to be, he was quick to stand up for them.

Unknowing to Carl Montgomery, he was the greatest benefactor of a friend like Bobby. Carl was the biggest kid in Denny's class, but in his case, biggest hardly meant the strongest or toughest. Carl was a klutz, and he

6

possessed a big, and often rather abrasive mouth that often landed him in trouble. Carl sometimes offended older kids in school, some of whom desperately wished to knock his block off, but knowing that he was tight with Bobby, they decided that it would be in their better interest to ignore him.

In spite of his many short comings, Carl had endeared himself to Denny, Shawn, and Bobby. He had an extremely active sense of humor, and if the other boys were bored when Carl was around they could dare him to do things. Carl was as gullible as they came and his friends had gotten him into all kinds of trouble by daring him to do things for their amusement. Big Carl seemed unable to turn down any of the challenges the boys put before him. It was like he felt that to turn down a dare would be a serious blow to his manhood.

On one occasion Bobby had dared Carl to go and take a shit in the girl's washroom. Whatever it was that Carl ate, it always caused the smell of his bowel movements to be extremely offensive. Young Mr. Montgomery seemed quite proud of this claim to fame and upon this dare, he first laughed hysterically at the idea of violating the girl's washroom in such a manner, and then without any further hesitation trucked right on in there without even bothering to first see if anyone was if there were any occupants in it.

As luck would have it, when Carl was leaving the washroom after dropping his bomb (not bothering to flush of course) Mrs. Witherspoon, who taught most of the subjects to the grade eight students went into the washroom. Mrs. Witherspoon was a nice enough lady, but she was known to have a weak stomach, All of the students knew of this and often played an assortment of tricks on her that they knew would be sure to make her gag. Bobby, Shawn, and Denny had been waiting in the hall where they had a good view of the door marked "GIRLS" when they saw Mrs. Witherspoon disappear inside. At first they were horrified, and then when they were struck by the hilarity of the situation, they laughed until tears streamed out of their eyes.

"What are you doing in here young man!?" Mrs. Witherspoon asked Carl sternly when she saw him exiting the stall.

Then before Carl could answer, his stench, worse than rotten eggs, struck her. Mrs. Witherspoon's nostrils flared and then she began retching violently. She wound up losing the lunch she had just finished all over the floor, some of which splattered onto Carl's shoes. It turned out to be the end of the day for poor Mrs. Witherspoon, the mere memory of the stench had kept her retching on and off for the remainder of the day. It was also the beginning of a week long detention for Carl.

Denny talked to both Bobby and Carl at school the day after his and Shawn's enrollment to confirm for himself that they really were in scouts. Satisfied that in fact they were, Denny's reluctance to attend eased.

That night, Shawn had brought a pamphlet to bed with him that listed the things that the Vollmer's Hollow scout troupe was going to be doing over the next little while. He kept a flashlight under his pillow so he could read comic books at night and he turned that on so he could see.

"We're going to do some neat stuff," he said.

"Oh ya," said Denny sarcastically. "Like watch Lester eat his snot, or better yet, how 'bout we watch Lester eat Johnny's snot? He does that you know."

That was enough to bring on a bad case of the giggles for Shawn.

Denny can be such a shit head, he thought.

Listening to his brother laughing in the bunk above him was enough to get Denny going too. He put his feet on the underside of Shawn's mattress and began bouncing him up and down. When he stopped, Shawn leaned his head over the side of the bunk meaning to hit Denny in the face with his pillow. Denny beat him to the punch however, and whacked his big brother with his own pillow. The blow almost caused Shawn to fall right out of the top bunk and the two of them laughed more loudly. A little too loudly.

"Get to sleep in there!" Their father warned from the living room.

The boys settled down, although it took them a while to stop giggling completely. When it had finally been silent for a few minutes, Denny whispered. "What kind of stuff are we gonna do?"

He could hear a rustling of paper and the click of a flashlight switch as Shawn pulled the pamphlet out again.

"The Saturday after next, we're going to the museum."

"Oh yay," whispered Denny, again sarcastically, "like we've never been there before."

Their parents had taken them there once, but neither of the boys had really been old enough to have understood anything that the guide had been telling them. Denny was just trying to be a difficult. As far as he was concerned, all museums were the same, and all of them were boring.

9

"Then on the first weekend of summer vacation, we're going hiking at Reid's Canyon. It says we're camping out there for three nights too."

"Really?"

"Yep."

There was another moment of silence. Shawn knew that Denny was letting that last bit of information sink in.

"Awesome!"

Shawn grinned. He thought that his little brother would like that idea.

The thought of camping out at the canyon caused Denny to look at the scouts with a much more open mind. He thought about Johnny and Lester too, and although he really did think that they were weird, it was always fun to laugh at them. Who knew what the Sabina brothers might do out there in the wilderness. It would be interesting to find out. Denny now found that he was actually looking forward to scouts.

3.

Mala stood on a small ledge looking up at the lip of the canyon wall. In her mind this ledge was hers, her special place. It was still within the boundaries of where she was permitted to go, but it was far enough away from everyone to allow her to feel alone and safe from the eyes of The Other. Sometimes she sat here for hours on end pondering all sorts of questions that flowed through her mind. Today as she sat gazing upwards thinking about what might lie outside the boundaries that had been imposed upon her people.

What could possibly be so terrible up there? Why should we fear outsiders so?

It was questions such as these that had eventually drove her to finally climb up there to see for herself. To outsiders, this climb would have looked treacherous, and an attempt to scale it without the aid of ropes or other climbing gear would have seemed fool hardy, but because their caves and tunnels were on the canyon wall, all of the Sasquatch Indians were excellent climbers. It was something that they had to learn to do just to get out of their homes to carry on with their daily business. If they needed food or water, or simply wanted to visit the community grounds they had to scale down the wall to get there. To them climbing was just as natural a thing to do as walking was.

Tonight Mala didn't remain on her ledge for long like she sometimes did. She was anxious to feel the sense of freedom she experienced every time she made her temporary escape from the canyon. Once at the top, even her thoughts seemed less restrained. Thoughts that when she was within the prescribed boundaries The Other was capable of intercepting. Mala had wrongly convinced herself that his powers didn't extend outside of the canyon. She was sure that this was the real reason he didn't want her or any of her people to stray too far. When she was up here there was grass and trees for as far as the eye could see. She could roam for miles and feel the cool, night dew on her bare feet without worrying about the boundaries like she had to when she was in the canyon. Down there she was only permitted to go a short distance away from the caves thus making her world so very small, a world that she was sure was much larger than she had ever dared to imagine.

Outsiders didn't venture into the Sasquatch Indian's section of the canyon very often, but they did come from time to time, and there was no way of telling when one of them might show up. This was the reason given them for the strict enforcement of their boundary laws. In the warmer seasons the risk of discovery was greater than in the winter, but they had to be careful all year round.

Mala walked in the darkness touching as many of the trees and plants she passed as she could. She stopped occasionally to pick flowers, gingerly touching their petals, feeling their softness and deeply inhaling their sweet aroma.

Why does The Other tell us that it's dangerous up here? She wondered. She had seen for herself that there was nothing to be afraid of, *and why does the chief listen to him?*

Mala knew the answer to this last question. The chief was afraid of him, just as all the other chiefs before him had been. The Other wasn't human, of this she was sure. Exactly what he was she didn't know. She knew that

12

in spite of his compact size he was extremely powerful physically, and he also possessed a vast knowledge of magic. This magic was never put on display for the tribe to see, but she knew it was there. It was something all of them could sense. The Other always knew things that he shouldn't. Sometimes he had knowledge of intimate details about some of the people of the tribe. All of them were sure that The Other could read minds.

But if that is so, then no matter how well I hide myself, he knows about me.

This thought was very disturbing. Mala's mother had given her stern warnings about The Other.

"It is best for young females to never let themselves be seen by him. Especially very pretty, young females such as yourself."

Mala had caught glimpses of The Other in the past. He was ugly. He appeared human ... almost. Although he was powerfully built, he was small for a man. His head was far too small even for his compact body, and it was framed by a wild mass of filthy, black hair. Mala had been told that a pungent odor followed The Other wherever he went. It was the smell of death and decay. Mala, who already needed no further reasons to fear him had listened to her mother intently and then asked, "why?"

"Because if he takes a shine to you he may want to take you as a bride once you have reached the age when you are eligible to marry."

Mala knew that The Other already had a few wives, and over the course of his lifetime, an immortal lifetime, he'd had many wives. Mala knew all about the physical relations between men and women. The Sasquatch Indians had never felt any need to keep such things a secret from children. It was a natural part of day to day life and

13

nothing to feel sheepish about. She also knew that in most instances, the women of her tribe enjoyed these relations just as much as the men did. All save for the wives of The Other.

Mala knew that something bad happened to the wives of The Other. She had seen them. They were just as free to interact with the rest of the tribe as anyone else, but their minds were gone. Whatever went on between them and The Other had driven them insane. Mala could imagine The Other's ugly little body being pressed tight against hers in the act of sex. She could imagine being unable to escape his stench, and how horrible it would be to have him inside her. It was no wonder that his wives went mad.

Two years earlier, just before Mala had begun to roam on the nights she felt it was safe, she had watched from a hiding place as The Other had taken on his most recent wife. She had known the young woman and had felt a great sense of pity for her as she watched the chief and two other men from the tribe drag her, kicking and screaming to the ceremonial altar where The Other awaited. Such behavior normally would have been cause for her to have been offered as a sacrifice. Any kind of defiance of either the chief or The Other always did, but Mala suspected that this wasn't the first time that one of The Other's brides had carried on in such a manner. Indeed she could understand it.

4.

The trip to the museum proved to be much more interesting than either Shawn or Denny had anticipated. The first time they had gone to the museum they had went with their parents while very young. They had been left pretty much on their own to wander around and look at the various displays, and they really hadn't known much about what they were looking at. This time however, they had a guide, an ancient lady who seemed to know everything there was to know about Vollmer's Hollow and it's history.

It was hard not to pay attention to this little old lady. She obviously loved to talk and she rambled on and on enthusiastically. Her entire presentation centered on rather dark tales of the good old days of yore in Vollmer's Hollow and it's surrounding area.

Denny and Shawn hated to admit it, but they found themselves afraid of her. How bad was that? A guy had to be a real sorry sack of a candy ass to be afraid of a little old lady. No matter how hard they tried to convince themselves otherwise however, they couldn't deny that the old bat had given them a serious case of the heebie jeebies. There was a disturbing aura about her. Her presence reminded Denny of an accident he had once seen on the highway during a trip to Tamarack with his family.

"Don't look," his mother had warned, but Denny had been unable to will himself to avert his eyes. He had seen a man in a blue dress shirt standing with two ambulance attendants. The entire left side of that blue shirt had been saturated with red. The man's arm hung in such a manner that Denny had been sure it had been severed in the accident and was being held up only because it was trapped in his shirt sleeve.

Denny hadn't been the only member of the Jackson clan to have gaped at this grizzly spectacle, all of them had, including his mother. It was something that none of them had wanted to see, but they had all been compelled to look anyway. Now as he looked at this old woman in the museum, Denny felt the same way. Something about the sight of her troubled him, but he was unable to look away.

When the scouts got a chance to talk outside afterwards, Denny and Shawn were somewhat relieved to find that they hadn't been the only ones to have been afraid of the old woman. It sounded like she had given the creeps to all of them. It was hard to pinpoint exactly what it was about her that they had all found so unsettling. She had yellowed teeth that were too big for her mouth, and there was something about her eyes that wasn't quite right. Those eyes looked full of tired wisdom like the eyes of a lot of other old people the boys knew, but there was something else. Denny felt that when she looked at him, she knew things. Things that she didn't have a right to know, like perhaps what color the underwear he was wearing were. Maybe she knew about that time him and Shawn had vandalized the old fish shanty they spent so much time fishing in front of. When the old woman began to speak. Denny felt her mental *hold* on him lessen. He was finally able to force his eyes from her and found the back of Bobby's flaming, red head much more comfortable to look at.

The scout troupe sat Indian style on the floor in a semi circle around a display where the old woman was standing. There was none of the usual fidgeting like there normally was when a group of boys such as this was

16

assembled. Nor did any of them make a sound as they were all drawn quickly and intently to what the old woman had to say.

"I suppose all of you know that Vollmer's Hollow was named after a man called Jake Vollmer," she began, but for many of these boys, it was the first time they had heard anything about this. "Jake and his band of settlers were the first white men to inhabit this area. Long before he was born however, there were people who had lived here. These people were of course, Native Americans, or Indians as most people refer to them. Many years ago, for reasons unknown a band of Indians strayed from their original tribe and wandered into the wilderness in hopes of finding a suitable place to begin a new tribe of their own. Unfortunately winter arrived before they found such a site and they had to set up a temporary home somewhere in the vast forest south of here.

Food was scarce in the forest, and during that winter a number of the Indians in this band succumbed to starvation and perished. The remainder of the group were forced to make a difficult decision. They could go on eating nothing until all of them suffered the same fate as those who had already died, or they could eat this new source of food that had suddenly become available to them. They chose the latter of the two options and ate the bodies of their deceased.

At some point during that winter in the forest, these Indians decided that human flesh was a desirable delicacy and even after they made it here near the lake where food was plentiful, they continued to practice cannibalism."

Some of the boys had heard a little about the Sasquatch Indians before, but they had only heard about them in little bits and pieces, and none of them had known that they had been cannibals. Cannibals, they thought, only came from far away places, places like Africa or the Amazon jungle. To think that the ground in their very own back yards had once been trod upon by real live cannibals was amazing.

The ancient woman went on. "I suppose that most of you boys know why this tribe became referred to by the name, "Sasquatch" Indians, but for those of you who don't, I'll tell you all again anyway.

For as far back as anyone can remember, the great wilderness between Vollmer's Hollow and Tamarack has produced a multitude of reported Sasquatch sightings, and I'm sure that you have all heard more than your share of bigfoot stories.

Anyway, through studies of artifacts and such that these Indians left behind, it has been found that they had revered the Sasquatch as a god, and they named themselves after him. This is why the entire forest that is now known as Sasquatch National Park was given it's name. The same thing goes for Lake Sasquatch on whose shore our very own town is situated.

Soon after the Sasquatch Indians had settled into their new home they received a strange visitor. The Sasquatch normally weren't very hospitable when it came to entertaining guests. As a matter of fact, they usually considered anyone from outside of their tribe to be a tasty delicacy. This particular guest however, was different. He was unlike anyone they had ever seen before. He was darker in color than they were and he had a compact, but powerful frame. He possessed a head that was too small even for his abbreviated size and it was framed by a wild mass of black hair."

18

The old woman paused for a moment. Her eyes scanned the group of boys in front of her with those strange, piercing eyes. It looked to Denny like she was looking *through* each of them trying to sense if she'd touched any nerves. He was sure that for a moment that he saw her upper lip curl into a slight smile.

She's really enjoying this, he thought. *And if she's scaring the crap out of us while she's at it, it's all the better for her.*

"The truth of the matter was that the Sasquatch Indians were all afraid of this strange visitor," the old woman continued. "They all believed that he had the ability to summon black magic. No one knows for sure why they thought this, but he must have displayed something to make them think this for he ended up staying with them, and he even held a high position within the tribe. Through their fear of him, it appears that this outsider had more authority over them than even their own chief."

The old woman ended her story abruptly here and then she changed the subject back to Jake Vollmer, but she was interrupted by a timid voice.

"What happened to them?"

It was Bobby who had asked the question, Denny was glad that he did, he wanted to know as well, and as he was sure that all of the other boys did too, but all of them except for Bobby had been too afraid to ask. The old woman smiled openly this time revealing way too many of those big, yellow teeth as she did.

"That's a good question, and to tell you the truth," she explained, "no one knows for sure what happened to them. It looks like they simply disappeared. For all we can tell, they just packed up and moved elsewhere. It isn't

19

impossible to theorize that they still exist somewhere out there in Sasquatch National Park. That park is enormous, and there's still a lot of area out there that no one has ever seen. If a smallish group of people such as the Sasquatch Indians decided that they wanted to keep themselves hidden out there they could do it."

All of the boys' imaginations were now swimming. Denny was sure that most of them would go home and have nightmares tonight.

"Now let's get back to Jake Vollmer," said the old woman. "As all of you probably already know, Jake was one of the first white settlers in the area. Our town, Vollmer's Hollow was named after him.

Why Jake would have led his group of people here in the first place really doesn't make much sense. The long trek through the dense forest and over the rocky terrain with wagons, live stock, women and children must have been extremely difficult to say the least. It would have been much easier for them to search for a place to settle in the south, but they did make it, and because of them, we are all here today.

After the little community was established, Jake's thirst for adventure again overtook him and he began to wander off on his own into the wilderness for extended periods of time. One of these treks lasted so long that the people of Vollmer's Hollow believed that something terrible had happened to him out there and that he had died, but he eventually did return, and with one less eye than he had left with.

It became apparent to the townspeople that Jake had gone completely mad during his latest absence. He rambled on with wild stories about a giant seagull. He claimed that this seagull had attacked him and taken his

20

eye. The people of Vollmer's Hollow found this tale to be rather amusing, but what they were really interested in was the contents of a tattered sack Jake had brought back from the wilderness with him."

The old woman held up a battered, green, canvas sack for all of the boys to see.

"This very sack was full of gold. Somewhere out there in what is now known as Sasquatch National Park Jake had found a gold mine.

Gold does something to people, often times bringing out the worst in them. The people of Vollmer's Hollow were no different than anyone else in this matter, and the news of Jake's find inspired a frenzy of greed. Some of the men in town planned to wait for Jake to make another trip to his mine and follow him, after Jake had led them there they could kill him and his gold would be theirs. Jake however, although maybe mad, wasn't stupid. He had anticipated that a reaction such as this was possible, and when he left town he did so in the dead of night.

With the aid of a tracker, a group of these men followed Jake's trail to as far as Reid's Canyon, but once they got there they lost all sign of him. Since then quite a few attempts have been made to find Jake's gold mine, but so far all of these attempts have been unsuccessful. Also many of the people who went out on these searches were never heard from again."

The old woman ended her presentation abruptly. As Denny sat at his place on the floor digesting everything he had just heard, he was overcome by the feeling that someone was watching him. He looked up and saw that it was the old woman who had been staring at him. When she saw that she had gained his attention she winked at him. Then she walked to a doorway near the rear of the room they were in and exited.

For some reason the old woman's gesture had shaken Denny. Being paid such special attention to by the strange old bird put an unsettling pang in his stomach, almost like someone had punched him there.

Denny looked around at the other boys sitting near him to see if any of them had noticed that wink. They were now all pre occupied with talks to one another. Then Denny saw Johnny and Lester Sabina. They were sitting a little ways back from the rest of the boys. It seemed that no matter where they were, or how many people were around, the twins always found a way to be apart from everyone else. They were looking at Denny now, smiling.

Those two freaks saw her wink at me, Denny thought. He could see a look of knowledge in their eyes, and Denny was sure that even though he himself didn't know what that wink had been all about, the Sabina twins did, and he felt angry towards them because of it.

The scouts were now free to roam around the museum at their leisure and look at any of the displays that attracted their attention, but all Denny wanted to do was go home.

What the hell is that crusty old bat picking on me for?

Denny meant to talk to Shawn about what had happened when they got home, but once they got there he felt a little silly about being so freaked out by the whole thing and changed his mind.

That night he had a hard time getting to sleep. He couldn't get the vision of that old lady and her oversized yellow teeth out of his head. He couldn't stop wondering what Johnny and Lester knew about her, and he couldn't

22

stop thinking about cannibals and lost gold mines. He imagined himself dressed like Indiana Jones looking for that mine.

Wouldn't it be awesome if I found it? He thought.

When Denny had left to go to the museum early that day, he'd had no idea of the profound effect it was going to have on him. After tossing and turning in his bunk for what seemed like hours, he tried to talk to Shawn, but Shawn was, as their mother would say, dead to the world. Denny envied him for being able to sleep.

5.

Eric Abel Jr. had a lot to keep his mind occupied during the three hour drive from Tamarack to Vollmer's Hollow. After his father's death a few years earlier, Eric Jr. had inherited a tabloid newspaper, and the junior Mr. Abel knew that his father would be rolling in his grave if he knew what had become of the tabloid over the last couple of years.

In life, Eric Abel Sr. had been fascinated by the bizarre. He had loved stories about unexplainable events and unbelievable human accomplishments. Throughout the years of his lifetime, beginning as a young teen, the elder Eric Abel had amassed a huge collection of newspaper and magazine clippings, as well as an impressive number of artifacts that had amazed him in one way or another. Extremely impressed by the Guinness Book of World Records, and Ripley's Believe It Or Not, and seeing their success, Mr. Abel decided that there was plenty of room for yet another tabloid that dealt with the bizarre. Thus was borne his brain child, Abel-y Uncovered. He had thought that using the little play on his last name was quite clever.

Eric Abel Sr. worked tirelessly on his baby, so much so that it put a huge strain upon, and eventually ended his marriage. In spite of his efforts however, the little tabloid he had created never gained the same success as Guinness or Ripley, but money generated from his passion had never been a priority for Mr. Abel. He had been exploring the unbelievable virtually all of his life for next to nothing, and he had been happy to do so right up until the day he died.

24

When Eric Jr. took over the reigns of Abel-y Uncovered, he had intended to continue on with the tradition that his father had begun. In the beginning he had stuck to the same type of stories that would have made his father proud. Stories of mysterious monsters, lost civilizations, and alien abductions had been Eric Sr.'s. favorites, and Eric Jr. used such tales as a base for the tabloid's continuation, but then he made the mistake of taking on a partner in an attempt to gain a wider readership.

The partner, a Mr. Raymond Stone, had been in the publishing business for quite a number of years. He owned a portion of the Tamarack Daily News, and more recently had started up a book publishing company that had been growing with each passing year. Raymond Stone had a lot of important connections to the publishing world including big distributors that Abel-y Uncovered had never had access to.

When Eric Abel Jr. had initially partnered with Raymond Stone all indications had pointed towards growth and recognition for his tabloid. He saw in Raymond a purely positive influence and anxiously jumped into the deal without considering the fact that Mr. Stone might have some editorial ideas of his own for Abel-y Uncovered.

At the beginning of the partnership, Eric still had full control over the tabloid, but Raymond wasn't satisfied with the sales numbers.

"A little tweak here, and a little tweak there," he had told Eric. "That's all we need to do to pick things up a little. We have to add a little new material to draw in new readers."

Eric found it hard to disagree with what Mr. Stone was telling him, after all, the man had a proven track record for success in the business, so far every project he undertook had turned to gold. Eric felt his heart climb into his throat however when he saw the first issue of Abel-y Uncovered containing some of Raymond Stone's "tweaking."

Raymond had sent a small army of photographers to either camp out at the doorsteps of a number of celebrities, or to stake out the favorite haunts of some of these well known personalities. This in itself wouldn't have been so bad, what was bad however, was the pictures these photographers came back with. It would appear that the main objective of their mission had been to capture these celebrities at their most unglamorous moments. The headlines accompanying these photographs were all of a scandalous nature.

In one particular set of pictures it looked to Eric as though the photographer had gone right up to the house of a well known action movie hero and had taken candid pictures of him through his windows totally unbeknownst to the actor. The pictures showed this action idol clad in women's undergarments. Eric could only imagine what such pictures would do to the man's career.

In another set, a glamorous songstress had been captured retrieving a newspaper from her front doorstep. Judging by her lack of make-up and the disarray of her hair, she had just gotten out of bed. Her headline mentioned something about the deterioration of her appearance due to an addiction to crack cocaine.

Eric groaned aloud when he saw what Raymond had done. He had taken his father's little tabloid paper that in the past had always made an honest attempt to find the truth to the mysteries of the world, and turned it into a weapon of slander.

26

The Sr. Mr. Abel had always hated publications such as these. He had never understood the human race's seemingly unquenchable desire to knock down the icons of success that they themselves had set on pedestals in the first place.

"Of all the mysteries in the world," Eric Sr. had told his son, "the human psyche is the greatest of all."

In spite of the distasteful subject matter in Stone's first version of Abel-y Uncovered the issue more than doubled the tabloid's previous best sales record. A monster had been let out of the closet, and Eric Abel Jr. didn't see how to get it back in. Since that first new edition, each succeeding issue exceeded the sales of the last. Eric had become a very wealthy man, but he was now ashamed to be associated with the publication that his own father had founded.

Eric had once been married, but like his father before him, his obsession with bizarre tales often kept him away from home. His wife had been unable to understand why he preferred to spend so much of his time away from her chasing after strange facts, and in the end the strain on their marriage had proved to bee too much. She filed for divorce, and Eric had let it go uncontested. The couple parted ways without ever having the family they had once planned for together.

One of the mysteries that his old man had been most fascinated by was the legend of the Sasquatch, or bigfoot as he was better known as. Eric Abel Sr. had talked on the subject numerous times with his son. The elder Abel had never come right out and said that he believed such a creature truly existed, but he had never said that he didn't believe it either. What he had said was that it was possible they existed, and it was possible for them to have concealed

27

themselves from humans, especially considering their apparent habitat in secluded forests and other untamed areas.

"Most scientists think that he's nothing more than a fairy tale," Eric Sr. had told his son. "They say that if he truly existed someone would have found a Sasquatch carcass by now. That sounds like a fair enough argument, but I hear that it is very rare for anyone to stumble upon a bear carcass, and we know that there are plenty of them around. If the Sasquatch is as intelligent and as human like as the believers say they are, then they would probably bury their dead."

His father's enthusiasm about bigfoot had rubbed off on young Eric and his interest in the legendary creature never did fade away completely. After a few years of watching the tabloid bearing his name drag people through the mud, Eric decided that it was high time that he try to do something to try to direct Abel-y Uncovered back towards the track that his father had intended for it. Perhaps some material on Sasquatch was a good way to start. Eric also needed to get away from Raymond Stone and his photographers for awhile.

Given it's name, it only stood to reason that Sasquatch National Park would be the location for many claimed encounters with the mythical monster. Eric knew that in all likelihood the vast majority of these reported encounters where either the products of overactive imaginations, or flat out lies. Each year however, there were sightings reported by seemingly sane and responsible people who had nothing to gain by making up bigfoot stories. In fact, Eric found that many of these more responsible sighters were very reluctant to mention anything about what they had seen at all for fear of ridicule.

It was the stories from these people that interested Eric the most. He also noted that in spite of it's small population, which was only a very small percentage compared to that of Tamarack, there were more sightings reported from near a little town in the north called Vollmer's Hollow than were from the big city even though both communities bordered on the national park

Eric concluded that if indeed the elusive Sasquatch did exist, his chances of actually finding one or finding substantial evidence of their existence, he would be better served if he were to check out the northern portion of Sasquatch Park towards Vollmer's Hollow.

6.

Though he realized that the chances of finding conclusive evidence of Bigfoot's existence were next to nil, Eric felt that at the very least he could amass a solid collection of stories in Vollmer's Hollow. Upon his return to Tamarack he could insist that these stories be published by Abel-y Uncovered, and thus with it's new and greatly expanded readership, possibly change the direction of the tabloid from Raymond Stone's version of it back to it's roots, and what his father had wanted it to be.

When he arrived in Vollmer's Hollow, Eric Abel Jr's legs and backside were stiff from the long drive. There was a motel in the little town, but at present all of it's rooms were occupied. Eric learned of a boarding house that had cheaper rates than the motel, and after some searching found a number for it. The phone rang on the other end five times, and just when Eric was about to give up, and old woman answered.

Eric expected to be told that all of the rooms of the boarding house were occupied as well, but was pleasantly surprised to find that there were vacancies.

"I'm afraid that I can't come personally to let you in," the old woman told him, "but I always keep a room key hidden in cases of emergencies such as this."

Eric breathed a sigh of relief. *I should have made arrangements for a place to stay ahead of time,* he told himself, but before now he'd had no idea that Vollmer's Hollow was such a draw for tourists.

"The key is behind a lamp on a buffet," instructed the old woman. "You'll find the buffet just to the left of the front door. You'll find the room number taped to the key. I can't remember which key I left there this time, but I think maybe it's 201. In any case you'll have to use the stairs on the right to get there."

Eric thanked the old woman, but before he could hang up and make his way to the boarding house, the woman began to chatter. Before he knew it Eric found himself listening to gossip about people he had never heard of before. He guessed that the woman was starved for someone to talk to as many old people are, and endured her ramblings. When he was finally able to get back to his car more than half an hour had passed by, and his ear was numb from holding the telephone up against it.

Eric had planned to take a nap when he got into his room, room 201 just as the old woman had thought, but after he had lain on the king sized bed for only a short while he decided that what he really wanted was a good, stiff drink. Besides, the room he was in had a rather eerie quality to it that was making him uncomfortable. As he had made his way to his room he had heard no signs of life in the big house.

I must be the only one here, he had thought, but then he remembered that it was only mid-afternoon and all of the other tenants were probably out doing whatever it was that tourists did in Vollmer's Hollow.

Eric drove to the business section of the little town and found a building with the sign, "Imperial Hotel" posted on it. He was taken aback a little when he walked inside.

Not exactly an inviting atmosphere in here is it? He thought.

It didn't look like cleaning was a high item on the priority list at the Imperial Hotel. He didn't feel like driving anymore to find a more tasteful place to wet his

31

whistle, and he figured that the alcohol would kill whatever might be lurking in the glass his drink was served in.

Better yet, he thought, *I'll just get a bottle of beer.*

Eric found a little table near the bar and sat down. After he was given his beer he sipped at it and looked around taking note of the half dozen other patrons of the establishment. He suspected that he could probably find most of these same people here at just about any time of any day. They all appeared to be very much at home in this dingy, little haven.

A dirty man sitting at the bar stared at Eric intermittently. It was making Eric uncomfortable and he finally stared back at the man openly.

"City feller," said the dirty man.

Eric nodded, thinking now that the dirty man had acknowledged him he wouldn't pay any more attention to him. Instead the man got up off of his bar stool and made his way to Eric's table where he promptly sat without bothering to wait for an invitation.

"My name's Carver, who are you?"

Eric gave him his name.

"What brings you to our neck of the woods?"

Eric decided that a multitude of Sasquatch stories must have been traded here at the Imperial Hotel over the years, and this dirty man probably spent enough time in here to have heard them all.

Now is just as good a time as any to hear some tales, Eric thought even though this Carver person hardly looked like the responsible source that he was looking for.

"I'm doing a little research on Bigfoot."

Carver smiled, surprisingly his teeth were white and even.

32

"We hear lots of Sasquatch stories around here," he said.

The afternoon quickly turned to evening, and then to night as Eric listened to Carver. To his surprise he found that he was even enjoying this man's company. In spite of his appearance, that of a wino fresh out of the gutter, Carver impressed him as being of considerable intelligence. Perhaps not of the academic sort, but as he listened to the dirty fellow he was sure that he could gain quite an impressive variety of interesting, back woodsy knowledge from the man.

As soon as Carver finished one Bigfoot tale he rolled right on to the next. Eric wished that he had brought a tape recorder with him. He knew that he would never remember everything that was being told to him, especially with the number of beers he had drank while he listened.

"If you were going to go out in an attempt to find a Sasquatch for yourself, where would you go?" Eric asked towards the end of their visit.

"Canyon," answered Carver without hesitation. "Most would tell you the woods, but I took a canoe down the river in the canyon once when I was a young teen and I know that something's not quite right down there."

"How do you mean?" Asked Eric.

"Noises," answered Carver. "Something mimicking birds and such. The noises were close to the sounds from real birds, but I was brought up in the woods and I could tell the difference. I was being watched while I was down there."

"Did you see anything?"

"No, but I know something was out there. A person can tell when he's being watched, and I'm not ashamed to tell you that I was getting scared."

33

"Where can I get a canoe?" Asked Eric.

"I got one," said Carver. "Rent it to ya cheap."

"You're on," said Eric.

Carver gave him instructions on where to pick up the canoe the next morning, how to get to the canyon, and where the best place was to start out from was.

Eric was pleased. He'd hardly been expecting to get a solid lead so quickly. The best he had hoped for was to hear a good story or two, but now he had a lead on where he might be able to experience a tale of his own first hand. Of course, chances were that he wouldn't find anything, but the worst that could happen was that he would have a relaxing canoe ride in a peaceful atmosphere.

Or at least that's what he thought.

7.

The next morning Eric awoke with a slight hangover. He felt rested enough, but he remembered that he had been plagued by strange dreams during the night, and the dreams had seemed all too real. The predominant dream had been the sound of a baby crying, Eric was sure that one had gone on for a long time. The other one had been shorter, but far more disturbing. He dreamt that he had woken and seen a rotund, middle-aged woman standing in the corner of his room glaring at him. He'd been startled to see her, but the fear that he had felt went far deeper than the simple shock of seeing a stranger in his room. He had never seen this woman before so he didn't know how his mind had conjured her up, but whoever she was, she was surrounded by an aura of evil. Eric wouldn't have been able to explain why he had felt this way, but he was sure that the woman had a dark and malicious heart just the same.

Eric shook both dreams off. *Just the effects of too much alcohol and sleeping in a creepy old house,* he told himself, and by the time he had gotten himself showered and dressed, he had forgotten all about them.

Eric got into his truck and found a little coffee shop on the Main Street of Vollmer's Hollow. He got himself a large take-out, and just as he was leaving it occurred to him that it might be a nice gesture to get one for Carver as well. He bought a second cup, and then he was on his way following the scratchy map the dirty fellow had given him the night before.

After going down a back street and then a dirt road for about half a mile outside of the town limits, Eric found

Carver's place. It was quickly evident what Mr. Clean did for a living. There was junk littered all over, old cars and car parts, farm machinery, and a large variety of other debris. Carver had to be in the scrap metal business, and by the look of this place, he had been at it for quite some time.

When Eric found the driveway amid all the clutter, Carver was quick to amble up to his car. "So you're going to go through with it are you?"

Eric nodded and handed Carver the coffee he had brought for him. Carver seemed quite pleased with the little gift.

"Ever driven one of these things before?" Asked Carver pointing to an ancient looking, red canoe lying at the side of the driveway.

"Yes," answered Eric. He didn't bother to mention that he hadn't been in a canoe since he'd been a teenager.

"Well you be careful down there, there's only a couple of rough spots, but one of them's really rough. You'll have plenty of warning though, as soon as you see the water speeding up you'll have to portage. Can't have you damaging my fine vessel here," said Carver grinning. Then he went over to the canoe and hoisted it up over his head. "This thing is a little cumbersome, but you look like you should be able to manage it OK."

Eric got out of the car intending to help, but Carver quickly strapped the canoe to the roof rack of Eric's car without assistance.

"What do I owe you?" Eric asked.

"This cup of coffee is payment enough," answered Carver.

Eric was sure that the man didn't turn down a chance to earn a buck very often, and his refusal for payment meant that he held Eric in rather high esteem.

36

"Now you're sure that you want to go through with this?" Asked Carver. "There really is something weird going on down there. I wasn't making all of that shit up."

"Yes, I'm sure," answered Eric. "I'm looking forward to the chance to get away from people for a while."

"Easy enough to understand, just remember to portage as soon as you see the water speeding up. Like I said, it only does that in two places and there's a rapids following both of them."

"I will," said Eric. "Thanks a lot."

As Carver watched Eric Abel Jr. back out of his driveway and head down the road, he didn't realize that he had just become the last person in the civilized world to ever see him.

8

The final bell rang and school was out for summer. Both Shawn and Denny had passed easily, drawing them each another year closer to the ever rewarding daily grind of adult employment. Those endless days of summer vacation and freedom were here at last.

School had let out on a Tuesday, and the Jackson brothers spent the first two days of their summer vacation partaking of their favorite activity, fishing in front of the old shanty. Friday came quickly and it was time to leave for the hike along Reid's Canyon with the rest of the boy scouts.

Mike Jackson had a surprise for his boys, "I'm coming with you."

Ncither Shawn or Denny knew what to make of this development. None of the other boys' fathers were coming. Denny could imagine the taunting voices already.

" You two are such babies that your Daddy has to follow you around everywhere."

After he'd had time to think about it though, Denny didn't think they would get much harassment after all. Him and Shawn had friends over quite a bit and all of them thought that Mr. Jackson was pretty cool as far as fathers went.

Mike Jackson owned a small logging company and had been working in the bush since he'd been a teen. The physical work and many hours outdoors had given him a rugged appearance and had kept him in very good shape. Shawn and Denny rarely ever heard any of that, "my dad can take your dad," stuff from other the boys in the school yard.

Often times when his sons had company over Mike would take all of the boys out in the back yard and knock baseballs around with a bat so they could practice catching fly balls and such. Once he had even built a ramp for the boys so they could do jumps over it on their bicycles. Then he set a couple of garbage cans and a lawn chair under the ramp to give them something to jump over.

As it turned out, that ramp hadn't lasted very long. Only long enough for Carl Montgomery to make his first and only jump. Big and clumsy, Carl bragged to the other boys that he secretly had his own ramp at home and could jump a lot father than any of them. The other boys were used to such tales from Carl and they knew that he was full of shit.

"Okay then Carl Kneivel," said Bobby. Then he set two more lawn chairs behind the ramp, "jump that."

Undaunted, Carl got on his bicycle and got it going as fast as he could, but he lost his footing on the pedals during his approach to the ramp. He had lost too much speed to clear the garbage cans and lawn chairs, but he went up and over the ramp anyway. He did a nose dive and hit the second garbage can. His bicycle flipped upside down and dumped Carl head first onto one of the lawn chairs.

Mike had been watching and was sure that the silly bugger had broken his neck. His face ashen with concern, he rushed over to Carl to see how the boy was. He found that Carl had managed to get his head wedged in the weaving of the lawn chair and couldn't get it back out. Mike could see that the boy's face was beet red with embarrassment, but other than that he seemed none the worse for wear. Mike tried to pull the chair off of Carl's head, but after a few attempts at this, and because of the strange squealing noises coming out of Carl as Mike tugged on the chair, he thought it easier to cut the weaving of the chair with scissors to rescue the clumsy, young fellow.

That proved to be the last jump anyone ever took off of the ramp that Mike had built. Carl's crash had scared him so badly that he had disassembled it that very night feeling very foolish for ever thinking that it had been a good idea in the first place.

Anyway, now Mike found himself with his mind set on coming to Reid's Canyon with Shawn, Denny, and the rest of the scouts even though he had no overwhelming desire to spend an entire weekend in the wilderness with a bunch of noisy young boys. He would much rather spend a Saturday afternoon with a cold beer in his hand watching football.

Mike kept his real inspiration for his decision to tag along a secret. He had read a disturbing article in the Tamarack News a few days earlier. The story he had read was about the leader of a scout group in the city who had been molesting some of the boys. The leader of the Vollmer's Hollow troupe was a weasely looking little man named Wade Purdy. Mike didn't think much of Wade to begin with, and he had a hard time understanding why a single man with no children of his own would be interested in spending so much time with young boys in the first place. After reading the article in the newspaper it was all to easy for Mike to picture Wade taking a little too keen an interest with the boys. Mike was pretty sure that if anyone ever touched Shawn or Denny he would have to kill him, and spending the rest of his life for murdering some ass hole who desperately deserved it wasn't very appealing to him.

At first Mike was just going to tell his sons that they couldn't go on the hike, but then he reasoned that that really wouldn't be fair to them. Instead he volunteered to act as a chaperone.

After making this decision, Mike talked to some of the other boys' parents and found that a lot of them were relieved that he was going. Most of them didn't trust Wade all that much either, at least not enough to feel comfortable about having their sons camping out for three nights with him. Some had been trying to come up with good excuses for telling their boys that they couldn't go just as Mike had.

9.

Lying awake in the cave that she shared with her mother, Mala pondered a lot of unanswered questions as she often did before letting sleep overtake her. Mala had more on her mind than usual tonight. Tonight there had been a feast. A feast was another distraction that allowed Mala a chance to roam, and again she had been unable to resist a taste of freedom when the opportunity had presented itself. When she had made it back to the cave tonight she had found her mother waiting.

"Where have you been?" Her mother had asked.

Mala had never been any good at lying. Instead she lowered her eyes and said nothing.

"When I saw that you weren't here I looked for you," continued her mother. "I couldn't find you anywhere. I know that you were somewhere that you shouldn't have been."

Mala's continued silence was all the answer that her mother needed.

"No more," Erenya said. "You know what will happen to you if you are caught don't you? Or even worse, what do you think will happen to you if an outsider sees you? You don't need me to remind you do you? If you are seen The Other will know. He always knows."

Mala didn't need a reminder. She knew all to well what would happen to her if she were to allow herself to be seen. Especially if she was seen while wandering outside of the canyon where she wasn't even permitted to go. She would become the next feast, that is what would happen to her.

42

These feasts were something that Mala didn't understand. She had never taken part in one, and she didn't plan on ever doing so. She found the whole idea of these feasts to be utterly revolting.

Mala had seen the latest prisoner that some of the hunters had brought back to the Sasquatch camp. She had heard that a man had been caught traveling alone down the river, and an overpowering curiosity had come over her. She wanted to see what an outsider looked like for herself, and what it was about them that caused her people to fear them so.

One of the caves in the canyon wall near the hidden community grounds housed a cage for captives of the Sasquatch Indians. Mala knew that the man would be kept in this cage until all of the necessary preparations for the feast were completed. Although no law had been passed, it was generally considered that this cave was off limits while a prisoner was being held, but Mala again threw caution to the wind, and when no one was looking she entered the cave.

Mala didn't know what she had expected to see, a large, wild man with fangs perhaps, what she saw however, left her more confused about outsiders than ever. To her the man seemed harmless. He had short, graying hair, and had a completely unthreatening aura about him. She had known what his fate was going to be of course. The same fate awaited all outsiders brought into camp. This being the first time that Mala had ever seen an outsider, she had looked at him closely and could see the fear in his eyes, but behind the fear, she could see a kindness. The poor man was terrified. He had no idea of what was going on or what was going to happen to him. She could also see that he wasn't all that different from the men of her own tribe. He

43

was a little paler, and he wore strange clothes, but she certainly couldn't see anything evil about him.

Mala was sure that the only reason her people felt that outsiders were evil was because The Other had told them so.

Why couldn't the chief see the truth? She wondered, but she knew the answer. The chief was afraid of him. It was The Other himself who was evil, not outsiders.

Mala's father, Takka, had known this. Two years earlier he had tried to convince the chief that they would all be much better off if The Other was to be gone once and for all. Before seeing the chief Mala's father had also spoken to a number of the other men in the tribe.

"They won't put us all to death if we stand together," Mala's father had told them. "I'm sure that many of you will agree that our lives would be much better if we weren't in constant fear of The Other. What advantages does his presence bring to us? None that I can think of. I'm sure that I'm not the only one who is tired of his reign of terror. It's high time we banded together and sent The Other on his way once and for all."

Many of the men he had gone to had indicated their agreement with him, but in the end, when it came time to go to the chief, they had all been too afraid. If they had gone with him, perhaps the final outcome would have been different, and perhaps Takka would still be alive.

Mala didn't know that it had been her that had really made her father decide to speak out against The Other. Also unbeknownst to Mala was that she was more than just pretty, she was exquisite, and her father had known that if The Other ever laid his eyes upon her he would want to claim her for a bride. He also knew what became of the

44

brides of The Other just as everyone did. He had seen enough of them, and they all wore that same permanently shattered look. None of them ever spoke, they seemed to be no longer able to. As a matter of fact, none of them seemed capable to do much of anything other than to walk around in a daze. Takka had been able to keep his daughter away from The Other's eyes, but he knew that it would be impossible to keep her hidden away forever, and if The Other ever saw her, Takka knew that as soon as her sixteenth summer came around, Mala would become yet another victim to whatever it was that went on in The Other's matrimonial bed.

As noble as Takka's intentions had been, his decision to go to the chief alone had proved to be a fatal mistake, and he became the main course for yet another of the tribe's feasts.

Mala remembered her father well and missed him dearly. Although the two had never spoken about The Other amongst themselves, Takka's daughter held the same opinion of him as he had himself.

10.

    The road to the canyon was full of twists and turns, and riddled with bumps and potholes. There was a long incline towards the end of it that eventually led to Reid's River. At the river the road ended in a gravel loop. The center of this loop was used for parking and had long been a popular make out spot for teens who cared to venture this far from Vollmer's Hollow for a late night necking session.

    To the right of the loop was another road, this one was very narrow and it really wasn't much more than a muddy path that led to a small campground. To the left a path had been trampled, and this was the direction in which the scouts would head into once they had all assembled. The path inclined sharply and anyone who followed it for roughly a mile would find themselves overlooking Reid's Canyon.

    Along with his sons, Mike Jackson had given Bobby a ride. Bobby of the flaming red hair and the insatiable interest in football. During the drive, Mike and Bobby had talked non stop. Both had a different pick of teams they thought would win the Super Bowl. Mike found the confidence Bobby held in the team he had chosen to be humorous. As much as Mike had tried to convince him why he thought that Dallas was the better team Bobby wouldn't be swayed. As far as Bobby was concerned, Cleveland had already clinched the championship lock stock and barrel, and the games that they would have to play to get there were nothing more than a formality.

    When Mike and the boys made it to the loop, they found Wade and a few of the scouts, including Lester and Johnny Sabina, already waiting there. The twins had caught a ride with the scout leader. Denny had wondered how they were going to get here, he couldn't ever remember having seen the twins' parents. For all he knew they didn't even have any.

They probably have them tucked away in a freezer down in the basement. Denny caught himself thinking.

Mike, Shawn, Denny, and Bobby got out of the car and before long the rest of the scouts arrived. When he was satisfied that everyone was present, Wade began to speak to the group in the most official tone he could summon. Mike found that it was taking a little effort on his part to keep himself from grimacing as he listened. He was glad that he hadn't left the boys, Shawn and Denny as well as the others, on their own to deal with this little prick for three days. He also decided right then that this was going to be the last outing his sons were going to take with the scouts. The more he listened to Wade Purdy the less he liked him.

"Well boys, here we are," Wade began. "I think you are all going to have a good time over the next three days, but before we begin we need to set a few ground rules.

First of all, I don't want any of you to be wandering off on your own. I want to be able to maintain visual contact with all of you at all times."

Especially when they're taking a leak eh Wade? Mike thought. Then he chastised himself. *Stop it Mike. You should at least give him a chance until he proves that there's something wrong with him.*

But no matter how hard he tried, he was unable to think of Wade as anything other than a little ferret of a man who had nothing better to do with his time than to spend it with a bunch of young boys who weren't even related to him.

47

"Second, when we get to the canyon," Wade went on. "I don't want to see any of you getting too close to the edge. It's a long way down to the bottom and I don't think I need to tell any of you what the result would be if someone were to fall over.

And last, there's to be absolutely no horseplay or rough housing. If any of you break any of these rules it will mean the end of this outing for all of us. We'll turn right back around and head for home. Do I make myself clear?"

Good grief, Mike thought. *What does the little weasel think this is? Boot camp?*

It wasn't so much what Wade had said that Mike had found to be irritating. All of the rules he had outlined made perfect sense. It was the cocky attitude and the tone he used when he talked to the boys that annoyed Mike.

He wants them to think that he's a real he-man. Mike was sure that Wade really didn't give a damn about any of the boys. He simply wanted to have a young audience that he felt he could easily impress.

Unlike his father, Denny had found nothing wrong with the way Wade had spoken. While the scout leader had been talking Denny watched Lester and Johnny. He wondered if they were capable of following the simple instructions Wade had just delivered. He knew that the Sabina twins weren't stupid. He knew what kind of marks they got in class, they were always near or at the top. That had surprised Denny at first. They always seemed to be so out of it. They never got involved in any of the games the other boys did during recess. They always kept so much to themselves, and when they did talk to others it was always about something weird. Then of course, was their little practice of eating bugs and things. Denny couldn't help but wonder what they talked about when they were alone in the school yard, or anywhere else for that matter.

Do they act that way at home? And what do their parents think about them?

11

"So how does someone go about filing a missing persons report in that little town of yours?"

Constable McClean already deeply disliked the jackass calling him from Tamarack. Raymond Stone had been mocking him and Vollmer's Hollow since the call had begun. He obviously felt that anyone who lived in a small town was of inferior intellect, and he did nothing to hide his feelings.

Alex McClean figured that the missing man was enjoying himself immensely in the absence of this Mr. Stone, perhaps so much so that he had decided to extend his stay in Vollmer's Hollow, and had intentionally neglected to tell this man of his new plans.

Constable McClean sighed, "missing man's name?"

"Eric Abel."

"Age?"

"Forty-four."

The Vollmer's Hollow police chief continued to ask questions until he had a complete profile of this missing Mr. Abel. When he was finished he had to grit his teeth to keep himself from screaming at Raymond Stone over his next remark.

"So you and your boys up there do know how to go about looking for a missing person don't you? You aren't just going to take that information I just gave you and file it away in a drawer are you?"

Alex felt like telling him that that was exactly what he was going to do, and then he and his "boys" were going to pile into their pick-em-up truck, load it with moonshine, and go out, get drunk, and shoot themselves some possum so's they could make themselves some fine possum stew. Instead he said, "we'll do everything we can to find him, and we'll be in touch with you as soon as anything develops."

Raymond Stone hadn't bothered to tell Constable McClean that he really didn't give a shit about Eric Abel's well being. What he cared was that Eric still held the controlling share of Abel-y Uncovered and that any of the tabloid's financial transactions required his signature. Raymond Stone was working on changing this, but for now he still needed Eric's okay before dipping into the ever increasing revenue generated by the magazine.

Alex McClean, or Constable McClean as everyone in town insisted on calling him, had been made chief of police two years earlier when he had made sergeant. In spite of his promotion, the people of Vollmer's Hollow continued to call him Constable McClean. Alex rarely ever heard anyone call him by his real name. "Constable" had replaced "Alex" as his given name ever since his arrival in the little town. He doubted that more than a handful of people here even knew what his real name was, and as far as he was concerned, that was just fine with him. The people of the town liked him, and he liked the laid back lifestyle of Vollmer's Hollow, and he liked the people who lived here. Constable McClean was a good man and he would have done well as a cop anywhere, Vollmer's Hollow, Tamarack, or anywhere else, but it was here that he intended to stay.

At the conclusion of the telephone conversation with Raymond Stone, Alex set the handset back into it's cradle. If he remembered correctly, every year two or three tourists went missing, most of them never to be found. He chalked it up as something that was bound to happen,

51

unavoidable really. Sasquatch National Park really was vast and wild, and with so many inexperienced campers and hikers venturing into it's dense forests, it was no wonder that some of them became lost. These disappearances only added fuel to the tales of the bigfoot monsters legended to inhabit the area. Alex was amused by these tales, but unless a Sasquatch reached out of the woods and grabbed him by the balls, he wouldn't believe any of them.

Constable McClean phoned the only real motel in town and asked the clerk there if Eric Abel had registered there. When the clerk told him he hadn't, he gave him a description of the man just in case he had registered under an assumed name. The clerk told him that they had no single men in their mid forties presently staying at the motel, but if he saw anyone who fit the description he would call Constable McClean immediately.

Alex hung up the phone. There was one more place to try.

The old woman who ran the boarding house seemed to be quite proud to announce that Eric Abel was indeed staying in one of her rooms. She said that she hadn't heard from him in a few days however.

"Hasn't paid me yet either," she said. "I hope he doesn't turn out to be a dead beat. He didn't strike me as that sort, but you just can't tell for sure these days can you?"

Constable McClean agreed with her and then rubbed his forehead as the old woman went on to tell him about other dead beats that she had encountered in the past. It was a long time before Alex could even ask, let alone get her permission to inspect Mr. Abel's room, and then it was some time longer still before the old woman stopped talking long enough to allow him to quickly say good-bye, and finally hang up the phone.

After letting himself into room 201 using a key the old woman had left behind a lamp in the foyer of the boarding house, Constable McClean made a thorough inspection of the room. He was looking for anything to give him a hint of Mr. Abel's whereabouts, but he saw nothing to indicate where it was that the man had disappeared to. An expensive looking suit and pair of shoes amongst a few other personal belongings had been left behind indicating that Eric did intend to return to the room at some time, but where he currently was was anyone's guess.

12.

After Wade had laid out the ground rules it was
time for him, Mike, and the scouts to begin their hike.
Wade had told all of them that he hoped that they would
make it as far as the waterfall today, that waterfall would be
a good spot to set up camp for their first night. With
everything said that needed to be said, the scout troupe, all
dressed in their little green uniforms and wearing their little
green caps were off.

A bunch of little green geeks, thought Denny, and
he couldn't help but laugh as the thought of how silly they
must all look came to him.

After they had been walking for a while, and the
boys had quieted after their initial, excited chatter, Denny
found his mind wandering. As he walked, it wasn't hard for
him to imagine that he and the others were a squadron of
elite soldiers making their way through enemy lines to
carry out a mission in which they had huge odds stacked
against them. When he got tired of fantasizing about that,
he imagined that they were a group of explorers in the
darkest depths of Africa. Denny had always had a vivid
imagination, and when he found himself getting bored he
could turn that imagination on whenever he wanted to just
like it had a switch.

The path that they were following didn't always
remain directly on the canyon's edge. In many places it
veered off a hundred yards or more when rock formations
or thick brush didn't allow for easy passage. At times there
were lengthy stretches when the hikers couldn't see the
canyon at all. Eventually though, the trail came back on

course allowing the boys and their chaperones a breathtaking view of this majestic wonder of nature.

The scout troupe walked on and on. Sometimes one of the boys would see something worth commenting on, like a hawk, or a snake, or a strangely shaped tree, and the whole group would yammer away loudly. All except for Johnny and Lester Sabina that is, who remained at the rear of the pack in silence.

As Wade had hoped, they made it to the waterfall late in the afternoon.

"Wow!" Exclaimed Bobby and some of the other boys when they came to it.

"Look at that!"

The waterfall really was something to see. A large creek had cut it's way through the canyon wall and then deposited itself into Reid's River far below. The boys automatically began to look for sticks and other debris that they could throw into the creek so they could try to follow it's progress down the falls.

"That'll be about enough of that!" Warned Wade. "I don't want any of you getting too close. If one of you falls in there will be no way to save you from going over, and you don't need me to tell you that it's a long way down."

The fresh air and long walk had tired the boys, especially the ones like Carl who had grown too accustomed to music videos and computer games. When the scout leader announced that they had come to the spot where they were going to camp for the night, almost all of the boys immediately unfastened their backpacks and let them plop to the ground. Getting them to go about the task of getting their tents up took a little persuasion, and Mike and Wade had to assist with more than half of them.

They got two fires going and roasted hot dogs over the open flames. Denny and Shawn didn't sit at the same fire as their father. Mike knew that this was because they wanted to feel that they were capable of trekking through the wild just like the others without any extra help from him. He hoped that his sons weren't finding his presence to be too awkward.

When it became dark, everyone huddled around the fires and soon campfire tales began to flow. The scout leader told Mike and the boys that sometime in the next day they would be somewhere in the vicinity of where Jake Vollmer's gold mine was believed to be. This of course started up tales that Jake's ghost was still standing watch over that mine.

Then there were tales about the Sasquatch Indians, and others about Bigfoot himself. Many of the boys were exhausted from the day's long march. These stories seemed to revive them a little, but once they all got tucked away into their sleeping bags it wasn't long before every last one of them was sound asleep. All of the trouble they had gone through to get the tents up now seemed to have been in vain because all of the boys had opted to sleep under the stars.

"At least they're already up and ready to be used if we get rain in the middle of the night," said Wade while him and Mike sat up for a while longer drinking coffee.

Mike was finding Wade's demeanor to be much more tolerable now that they boys were all asleep and Wade had no one left to try to impress. Johnny and Lester Sabina weren't far from where the two of them were sitting and Wade watched them sleep for a while.

"Those two are rather odd, don't you think?" Wade asked.

Mike smiled. He had thought so as well, but hadn't thought it was something that he should say out loud, and after what his initial impression of Wade had been, Mike found it humorous that the scout leader should be calling anyone else odd.

"I suppose your boys have talked to you about them," Wade went on.

"Ya, I've heard some things," said Mike.

"You ever hear about their diet?"

"You mean the bugs and things?" Asked Mike chuckling a little.

"Yes," answered Wade. "What do you suppose possesses them to do that?"

"Who knows, it's probably just one of those boy things. You remember what it was like don't you? Sometimes we liked to try to gross everyone out. It probably just seems odder to everyone when those two do it because they look alike and keep to themselves so much."

"Ya, I suppose," said Wade. As he watched them he could tell that Johnny and Lester were both dreaming, and by the way their heads were both rolling back and forth he didn't think either of them were having a pleasant one. "Look at that," he said.

Mike looked. Watching the two of them that way was kind of creepy.

"How much do you want to bet they're having the same dream?" Said Wade

After watching Lester and Johnny for a while longer Mike didn't doubt that that was exactly what was going on.

"Those two boys are really odd I'm telling you," said Wade. "I wouldn't even be surprised to find out that they can read each other's minds. Have you seen the way they stay away from everyone all the time? And they hardly ever talk to each other. I bet they're talking up a storm in their minds though."

"I've heard talk about twins being able to do that between one another before," said Mike. He wasn't convinced that Lester and Johnny could do that, but this conversation was interesting. "I saw something about it on TV once."

"I've heard the same things," said Wade. "But sometimes when I'm around those two, I think that they can tell what's going on inside my head as well. It really is rather unsettling."

Mike understood exactly what Wade was saying. He had to admit that there had been times throughout the day when he had felt exactly the same way.

13.

Denny woke in the night. Everyone around him was asleep and the darkness was silent. Or was it? He thought he could hear a faint noise in the distance, and a moment later he could clearly hear a sound coming from somewhere in the forest around him. The crickets were constant and there was an owl nearby hooting at irregular intervals. Then the owl was quiet and even the crickets seemed to have suddenly become a little less rambunctious about their chirping.

The new sound which had been soft and hard to identify at first finally became familiar to Denny and he realized what it was as it came closer -- flapping wings, very large flapping wings. Whatever it was that was flying out there seemed to be circling the camp. It remained wary enough to keep at a distance for a while, but when it came closer Denny's eyes grew wide. He had watched enough vampire movies for his imagination to put pictures of a huge bat soaring around them into his mind -- perhaps this bat was trying to decide who amongst the scouts was the most vulnerable, which of them was the most likely source for it's next taste of blood. Then as whatever it was in the darkness above flew directly overhead Denny pulled his sleeping bag up over his head.

Just a bird, He tried to tell himself. *Just a bird.*

Then the thing let out a loud, piercing cry that sent shivers along Denny's spine. He had heard that cry before, but never so loud, and the birds that this cry usually came from never got to be nearly as big as the one that had just flown over seemed to be.

Denny could hear others from the group stirring, the loud sound had disturbed their sleep. He couldn't tell if any of them were fully awake or not and he didn't bother calling out. He just laid where he was in silence and listened to the night until he was satisfied that the bird was gone.

14.

Everyone was up early the next morning. No one mentioned anything about strange bird calls in the night. The boys were excited to make bacon and eggs in a cast iron frying pan over open flames. Even the ones who preferred sugar saturated cereal for breakfast ate what they had cooked with greater relish than if the same thing had been prepared for them at home. Truthfully, bacon and eggs at home would have tasted much better. The eggs were somewhat blackened with ashes from the fire and the bacon had a strong, burnt flavor.

The plan for the day was to make it to a spot where Jake Vollmer had once been rumored to have been sighted many years ago. Many people in Vollmer's Hollow still believed that his gold mine was in a hidden location somewhere along the canyon in the area that this supposed sighting had taken place, but no one had ever found it.

The scouts and their chaperones would camp out at this site and then turn around and head for home. Already some of the boys had grown tired of this wilderness game and their progress was slow. Some of the more enthusiastic young explorers began telling stories about Jake that they made up as they walked. Most of them involved Jake's supposed ghost maiming or killing anyone who stumbled too close to his mine.

Denny hadn't mentioned anything about what he had heard in the night yet, but as the tales went on he couldn't contain himself from throwing a story of his own into the fray any longer.

"The shit hawk that took Jake's eye watches out for him now," he said.

Mike wanted to warn his son about using such language, but then thought better of it. *Boys will be boys,* he thought. Mike called the birds in question shit hawks rather than sea gulls himself. He had probably used the term dozens of times while in ear shot of his boys and that was probably where Denny had picked it up from in the first place.

"That seagull is a giant one," Denny went on. He flies all around watching people. Most of the time just around the canyon looking for anyone who gets too close to the mine, but sometimes he goes right into Vollmer's Hollow. Then he flies back to Jake to let him know what he sees."

Denny was well known for making up entertaining stories at school. Many of the boys here were classmates of his and they were fully enjoying this new tale.

"Your boy's got quite an imagination," Wade said to Mike.

"Ya," Mike grinned. "I guess he does doesn't he. He's always making up stuff like that at home too."

"Maybe he'll be a writer one day," said Wade.

"Maybe," agreed Mike.

As they walked Lester and Johnny Sabina remained at the rear of the pack just as they had the previous day. Sometimes they walked closely together and other times at a distance from each other, but they always remained a constant distance behind everyone else.

As time wore on Mike was finding that the twins made him feel more and more uneasy. At times he could almost feel a hole being bored into his back by two pairs of eyes.

Why should I let a couple of kids get to me like this?
He asked himself. *What exactly is it about them that
bothers me?*

Mike didn't have an answer to his own question.
Whatever it was he couldn't quite put his finger on it. He
had watched from a distance during a break earlier in the
day as Bobby dared Lester to eat a caterpillar. When Mike
had first realized what was going on he had intended to go
over to the boys and put a stop to it, but a somewhat morbid
curiosity overcame him and he wanted to see for himself if
it was true that the twins would eat bugs. He was mildly
amused as he watched Bobby rummage through his pockets
for some change. A couple of the other boys had noticed
what was going on and they went over to watch the show as
well. When it appeared that Bobby couldn't find a quarter
Carl produced one and handed it over to Bobby who in turn
handed it over to Lester. Lester slipped the coin into his
own pocket and then held out his hand to let Bobby drop
the caterpillar into it. Mike was sure that he heard Bobby
telling Lester something about having to chew it, and then
without hesitation Lester popped the caterpillar into his
mouth. He held it in his lips for a moment letting part of
the bug squirm around under his nose, and then he stuck
out his tongue and swiped the whole caterpillar into his
mouth with it. Once he had all if it in Lester began
chewing just as Bobby had instructed.

Mike imagined the green guts squirting out of the
caterpillar and thought about how awful it must taste.
Unconsciously an expression of amused revulsion came
over his face.

That fucking kid is nuts, he thought. *That was
really gross.*

63

Then he noticed Johnny a few paces away from Lester and the onlookers. Johnny was staring directly at Mike and a funny sensation came over him.

Johnny's reading my thoughts.

However unbelievable that idea seemed to him, Mike knew that that was exactly what was happening. Then Johnny looked over at Lester and Lester immediately glanced back at Johnny and then both of the twins looked over at Mike.

Both of them are.

Mike suddenly found himself too uncomfortable to look at them any more and he got up and went looking for Wade. He needed another adult to talk to, even if it had to be one that he didn't particularly like. He wasn't going to say anything about his suspicions of the twins reading his mind, he just wanted to think about something else. As he walked he found himself trying to keep his mind blank.

Later that afternoon, the group reached a spot that looked like a good place to set up camp for their second night. Wade and Mike again instructed the boys to set up their tents.

"Can't we just sleep under the stars again?" Bobby asked.

"Yes, but you have to set up your tents anyway."

"What for?"

"Just in case it rains."

All of the boys looked up at a cloudless sky.

"It doesn't look like rain."

"No, and it probably won't rain, but if it does you'll be happy that you had them set up."

With only a little grumbling the tents went up, once again with a lot of help from Mike and Wade.

64

15.

Constable McClean took the photograph out of the envelope. He had been expecting its arrival and was happy that Raymond Stone had been quick about sending it, he wanted to show it around town before too much time had elapsed and people's memories faded.

Alex studied the photograph of Eric Abel. He looked like a pleasant enough fellow. He had an open face and friendly eyes under a full head of gray hair.

So where have you gone to? Constable McClean wondered. He was no closer to finding this man now than he had been when he had first heard of him.

During the next couple of days, Alex McClean carried the picture around with him wherever he went, and he showed it to as many people as possible. No one could remember having seen Mr. Abel. Alex didn't find this as any great surprise, Eric hadn't been in town very long, and like people in many small towns, the inhabitants of Vollmer's Hollow liked to keep to themselves paying attention only to those faces that were well recognized. Tourists were received cordially enough, but for the most part were ignored by the locals as far as any sort of social interaction went.

By the time Constable McClean made his way into the Hollow Pit with his photograph he had all but given up any hope of finding Eric Abel. He showed the picture to the scruffy looking lot of regulars in the bar, but none of them could remember seeing him.

Carver had seen the photograph that Constable McClean had been showing around, and he had recognized the man he was looking for.

Well the silly bastard, Carver thought. *I warned him didn't I? I asked him if he was sure he wanted to take a trip down the river. If he's gotten himself lost down there it's his own damn fault. It's none of my doing.*

Carver was also still pissed at McClean for locking him up one night. Carver had been very drunk on the night in question, and he had walked out of the Imperial Hotel, better known to locals as, "The Hollow Pit," and onto Main Street. There he unzipped his pants, and pissed in the middle of the road. A number of people had seen this display including a couple of young children, and Constable McClean himself. Alex had offered to give Carver a lift home, but the drunken man had told him to fuck off.

"I'm perfectly fine to drive home myself occifer," he had said.

Constable McClean didn't doubt at all that Carver would at least try to do just that and he thought would be safer for everyone in town, including Carver himself, if he were to first sleep off the alcohol before driving home.

After Alex had finished showing his photograph around and left the Hollow Pit, Carver remained perched on his regular stool at the bar drinking a little more quickly than usual. It had been very much unlike him to talk to an outsider, but he had enjoyed talking to Mr. Abel and now he was feeling guilty for not acknowledging that he had recognized him in the photo.

Why should I help that McClean? He thought. *Lock me up in jail and then ask me for help? I don't think so.*

Carver didn't remember peeing on Main Street or insisting that he drive himself home that night, and even if he could remember he probably still would have thought that the police chief had been in the wrong.

When Eric Abel had failed to return the canoe, Carver suspected that something was wrong. He knew that Eric wasn't the sort of man who stole things, especially something like that beat up canoe. He should have been back long ago.

Shouldn't ever have lent the damn thing to him, but how was I supposed to know this was going to happen?

Carver continued to drink and tried without much success not to think about the whole mess. *McClean might as well give up,* he thought. *If that guy's been down there this long, there's nothing anyone can do for him now.*

16.

After the boys had eaten beans and wieners for dinner and the sun had gone down, the group again divided itself amongst two separate fires. Most of the boys around one, and Mike and Wade at the other. Some of the boys wandered back and forth between the two. Lester and Johnny sat a ways back of both fires in the shadows alone together as always.

More ghost stories were told. Even Mike got into the act by telling the classic urban legend about the escaped psycho patient who had a hook in place of a lost hand and lurked about a popular make-out spot.

Wade took his turn by again reminding everyone about Jake Vollmer and his gold mine.

"We are now very close to the last spot Jake Vollmer was ever reported to have been seen ... alive. Since then it has been told by more than one hiker that old Jake's ghost can be seen roaming about in this area from time to time. Some people say that Jake had been shot and killed by a group of men who were after his gold. That was rather foolish of them don't you think? Because when Jake died he took his secret of the location of his mine away with him forever. As a matter of fact, the very spot where we are now camping could very well be the site of his murder."

Mike had to laugh to himself when Wade finished his story. He could see by the look on many of the boys faces that the scout leader had struck a nerve. Mike himself could sometimes have a rather twisted sense of humor and he could now see that Wade did as well.

Maybe the little twerp isn't such a bad guy after all.
Mike thought. He wondered how many of the boys would
be having nightmares tonight. He wouldn't be surprised if
there were a few.

Curiously, Denny Jackson didn't have anything to
say. He was a huge fan of spooky, old fashioned, camp
fire, ghost stories, and it was very much unlike him not to
try to out do everyone else with a tale of his own.
Although Denny liked to make up scary stories, apparently
when he had a real life experience he was reluctant to talk
about it. The story he had told earlier in the day about the
giant shit hawk had already slipped the other boys' minds,
but Denny remembered.

As the time drew near for everyone to go to sleep,
Denny's mind was occupied with the thought of the large,
flapping wings he had heard the night before. In his silence
he was wondering what he might hear in the night this time.

When the boys crawled into their sleeping bags, all
of them fell asleep quickly. Two days of marching about in
the great outdoors had tired them out thoroughly.

All of them had fallen asleep quickly. All of them
that is except for Denny Jackson. He laid in his sleeping
bag with his ears peeled for sounds from the darkness. A
couple of times he convinced himself that he could again
hear giant wings flapping in the distance, but if that was
what he was hearing the bird that belonged to the wings
never came close enough for him to be one hundred percent
sure.

Finally, after he had convinced himself for the
fourteenth time that everything he had heard the night
before had only been a figment of his overly active
imagination, and just when he was about to drowse off,
some movement caught the corner of his eye to let Denny

know that perhaps he wasn't the only one in the group who had been unable to sleep after all.

Slowly he rolled his head over into the direction of where the movement had come from. He didn't want whomever was awake to know that he was watching them. A figure was standing in a crouched position on the far side of the camp from him. Then another emerged from his sleeping bag to join the first. It was Lester and Johnny, their platinum blonde hair made them unmistakable.

I wonder what they're up to, thought Denny. *They probably have to take a piss,* but as he watched a while longer he saw that they seemed to be acting with just a little too much stealth for it to be just that.

Then the twins began to creep to the edge of camp towards where the canyon lay a short distance away. Denny remained motionless watching them as they headed off into the shadows. He wanted to see what they were up to, but he didn't like the idea of trekking about in the dark knowing that somewhere out there was the owner of the giant, flapping wings. His curiosity overcame his caution however, and he decided to follow them. He had almost finished climbing out of his sleeping bag when a hand clasped his arm. Denny's heart jumped into his throat. He was so surprised that he almost screamed, but then he realized that the owner of the hand was his brother Shawn.

"You gonna follow them?" Shawn whispered.

Denny nodded.

"I'm coming too."

Shawn slipped out of his sleeping bag, and together the two boys crept away into the darkness after Lester and Johnny.

Once outside of their camp Denny noticed that the moon was out tonight and glowing brightly. It wasn't full, but it wasn't too far from it, and it wasn't nearly as dark away from the firelight as he had expected it to be. Denny and Shawn continued walking. Occasionally they could hear small animals scampering away from them. The wilderness at night was strange, different than in the day. At night it seemed a secret place and both boys couldn't help but feel as though they were somehow trespassing into territory where they weren't wanted.

As they neared the edge of the canyon, Shawn nudged Denny and pointed to the left. Denny could see two platinum heads about seventy yards away. In the moonlight, those heads almost glowed. Denny could remember some of the kids at school joking that the twins' hair would glow in the dark and now he could see first hand that they hadn't been too far from the truth.

It appeared that Lester and Johnny were following the canyon edge. Every once in a while they would stop and look up towards the sky. They seemed to be either watching or listening for something.

That thing that was flapping around last night is probably those two freaks' pet, Denny thought.

"I wonder what they're up to," whispered Shawn.

Denny looked at his older brother and shrugged. "They're just being weird as usual," he answered.

Then in unison the twins turned and faced into Shawn and Denny's direction.

They're onto us, Denny thought, and he found it extremely unsettling to think that the Sabina brothers knew that they were being followed.

They'll know exactly who it is that's following them too.

Quickly though, Denny realized that it wasn't him and Shawn that the twins were looking at. Their gaze was

71

turned to the sky and slightly to the right of Shawn and Denny. Then hearing the sound of flapping wings approaching, Denny knew what had attracted Lester and Johnny's attention. There was a loud screeching sound from above. The piercing squeal of a sea gull is somewhat annoying at the best of times, but the high-pitched wail coming from this bird sent piercing waves seemingly right into the center of Shawn and Denny's brains. Unconsciously they both put their hands over their ears in an attempt to filter some of the sound.

The shit hawk ignored Shawn and Denny, going past them towards the twins. Then it swooped down and almost touched the platinum heads. This was the first good look Denny had gotten of the bird, and just as he had suspected, this sea gull was enormous. It was way too big to be any normal sort of shit hawk that he knew of and it's eyes glowed a furious red.

At first Denny thought that it was attacking the twins, but after swooping it once again flew high over head and out of sight. It looked however, as if Lester and Johnny were still able to follow it's progress and they turned into the opposite direction of Shawn and Denny and back somewhere a little distance away from them along the edge of the canyon. The twins looked at each other briefly and then began walking into the direction of where the shit hawk had flown.

This is just way too weird, thought Denny. It appeared that the giant sea gull was leading the Sabina brothers to somewhere in the canyon.

Denny and Shawn followed from a distance. Whether or not Lester and Johnny knew that they were being followed, neither Shawn or Denny could tell. It wouldn't have surprised either one of them if the twins had known all along. The Jackson brothers had long been convinced that the two of them could read minds.

Denny and Shawn had just come to a boulder when they heard the gun shot. Both boys hit the dirt.

"Sons of bitches!" They heard a voice full of sandpaper call out. "This is my claim! You squatters can just turn around and head right back into town."

Denny and Shawn huddled as close to the boulder as they could get. They would have crawled right inside of it if it were possible. They could hear a metallic clicking sound. Denny dared to peer around the edge of the boulder. At first he saw nothing, but then seemingly out of thin air, a figure appeared. It was a man loading a rifle. The man was perhaps sixty years old and he looked dirty and unkempt. Unlike many men of his age who were balding, this man had a full head of white hair that looked as if it hadn't seen a comb or shampoo in years. The clothes that clung to his wiry body didn't look like they had been washed in a very long time either.

The man's attention was drawn to something in the trees ahead of, and to the right of Denny and Shawn's hiding place. The man lowered his rifle and fired into the trees. Denny could hear another man's voice cry out in pain.

Holy shit! He just shot someone, Denny thought.

"How do you like that you dirty bastards?" Cackled the man with the rifle.

He was answered by a short barrage of gun fire coming from the trees. It sounded like there were a few more men out there yet. The old guy stood unflinching right out in the open, but miraculously he didn't get hit by any of the bullets. Denny watched him look around for cover and when he spotted the boulder Denny quickly jerked his head back the other way. He pressed his back up against the big rock as tightly as he could, his eyes wild with fear. Shawn had heard everything that had been going on as well and he laid as still as he could afraid even to breathe.

The boys could hear footsteps approaching and then the sound of someone falling to the ground nearby, and then a wheezing. The old guy who was now sharing their boulder apparently had a badly congested chest. They could hear him hack and spit, and then there were more metallic snapping and clicking noises as he reloaded his rifle. Now with new ammunition in his gun the boys could hear him moving. He was rounding the boulder and coming right towards them probably in an attempt to find a place where he could get off another round at the men in the trees. Shawn and Denny were both frozen with fear. They didn't want to move from the boulder for fear of drawing fire from the shooters in the woods, they also didn't want the "wheezer" to see them either, but they had no where to go to get away from him.

Not knowing what else to do, the boys stayed rooted to where they were and looked with wide eyes in the direction of the approaching sound. The first thing that they saw was the business end of the rifle and they both closed their eyes tightly as if by doing so they could make everything simply go away. Then the sound of movement stopped. After a few seconds of silence Denny opened his eyes. The old guy hadn't gone away as he had hoped, but for the moment he didn't seem to be a threat.

The first thing that Denny noticed about the face looking at him was the missing left eye. In an instant Denny knew who it was that he was looking at. It was Jake Vollmer. He was sure of it. They had been reminded only

74

a short time ago that they had camped near to where Jake's gold mine was rumored to be, and he remembered all too well that spooky old lady in the museum who had told them about how Jake had gone mad and returned to town after one of his treks into the wilderness claiming that a giant sea gull had ripped an eye right out of his head. Now here they were face to face with a wild looking man with nothing on the left side of his face but a dark socket where an eye should have been.

But how could this possibly be Jake? Denny wondered. *The real Jake Vollmer would have died a long, long time ago. If this really is Jake, then it's his ghost.*

Anther thing that Denny noticed about the face was that it wore an expression of utter confusion. Finally the man spoke in a raspy voice.

"Who the hell are you?"

Then Jake looked Denny and Shawn over with his one good eye. He seemed to be finding their clothing odd.

"You're not supposed to be here," he said. "It's not your time yet."

Then the confused look on Jake's face turned to one of fear. He dropped his rifle, stood up, and began to back away from them.

"It's not fair," he went on quietly. "This can't be right."

Jake stopped back peddling and looked down at himself. He touched his legs.

"I'm right here," he said. "It's still my time."

He looked back up at Shawn and Denny. His fear had turned to panic.

"Get out of here!" He yelled. "It's not your turn! This is still *my* time! You're not supposed to be here! Do you here me?!"

75

Denny and Shawn were both too scared to do anything other than gape at the one-eyed man in horror. Then Jake turned on his heel, took a couple of strides as if he were about to run, and vanished.

"It just isn't right. It's still my time," the boys heard again, and then the night was quiet.

Denny and Shawn sat where they were for a while longer in silence trying to digest what had just happened. Finally Shawn spoke.

"Do you think he's gone?"

Denny shrugged, "I guess so."

"What about those guys in the woods?"

"I think they're gone too," answered Denny.

"What do we do now?"

"Go back to camp I guess."

"Where do you think Lester and Johnny went?"

Denny looked around the edge of the boulder again to make sure that the coast was clear.

"I don't know," he answered. "I Can't see them. Maybe they already went back to camp."

"Do you think they saw Jake too?" Asked Shawn.

"Who knows," said Denny. "Let's go back."

"What are we going to tell everyone?"

Denny thought for a moment before answering. "I don't think I'm going to tell anyone anything. They'd just think that we were making it all up anyway."

The boys got up and headed back towards camp.

"Hey Shawn," Denny said after they had walked a short distance.

"Ya?"

"That was kind of cool wasn't it?"

Shawn had to smile, *leave it to my little brother to find something that had scared the shit out us to be cool,* he thought.

They were walking along a narrow trail with small trees, shrubs, and tall grass bordering it along both sides. Denny stumbled on something in the trail and fell flat on his face.

"Quit screwing around," said Shawn.

"I'm not screw ...," Denny began, and then he saw her.

It's odd how things work out sometimes. If Denny hadn't fallen precisely where he had he would have missed her completely. The girl he was looking at was roughly his age, and even in the dim moonlight and shadows, Denny was sure that she was the most beautiful girl that he had ever seen. She was obviously Indian, and she wore a wreath of little white flowers in her long, raven hair. She had copper colored skin, high cheekbones, and big liquid brown eyes. He found her eyes to be fascinating and he was immediately drawn to them. Those eyes seemed so full of wild, vibrant life that it was easy to get lost in them.

The girl had been hiding, crouched down in the tall grass. Now that she had been discovered she stood and Shawn could see her as well. Both boys could see that except for a small loin cloth she was naked. Denny could see her budding breasts and she did nothing to try to cover them. The sight of her sent warm tingles through the private parts of his body and he was unable to look away from her. Shawn also seemed mesmerized by her and both boys were unable to do anything but look at her in awe. A hint of a smile touched her lips, and then she darted off, silently disappearing into the small trees and shrubs with such speed that Shawn and Denny knew it was hopeless for either of them to try to match.

"I wonder what she's doing out here?" Said Shawn while the two watched the brush for any further signs of movement.

Denny had been profoundly affected by the girl. The images of her beautiful face and her nakedness when she had stood were now forever burned into his memory and for the moment, as far as he was concerned, nothing else in the world existed. He could hear Shawn talking to him, but he had no idea as to what he was saying.

"You okay Denny?" Shawn asked.

Denny did nothing to acknowledge his brother, he simply stood where he was in a stupor.

"Earth calling Denny," Shawn said as he put his hand on Denny's shoulder and gave him a light shove.

Denny snapped out of his daze. "I wonder what she's doing out here?" He said.

Shawn rolled his eyes. "That's what I just said to you ya bone head."

"Do you think she's all right?" Denny asked.

"I dunno," answered Shawn. "She looked fine to me, and if something was wrong, I don't think she would have run away from us."

Denny figured that his brother was right about that, *but who the hell was she?* He wondered, *and why is she running around in the woods at night without any clothes on? Is she a ghost too? There's a lot of weird shit going on out here.*

We'd better get back to camp and try to get some sleep," said Shawn. "We've got to do that hiking thing again tomorrow and it's going to suck if we're really tired."

78

Denny nodded. Reluctantly he quit scanning the bush in his hopes of catching another glimpse of the girl and the two boys made their way back to camp. When they got there, they immediately slipped back into their sleeping bags. Before drifting off to sleep both boys looked over to where Lester and Johnny's sleeping bags were. They couldn't tell if the twins were in them or not.

17

Her mind overflowing, Mala lay awake in her cave with her eyes open, but unseeing in the darkness. Much had happened during the night that had just passed, and she didn't know what the consequences were going to be from any of it.

First she'd been seen by outsiders. This in itself hadn't worried her -- at least not right away. The outsiders had been young, close to her own age. She had been amused by their reaction to her and she had liked the way they had looked at her. She had temporarily forgotten all she had been told about outsiders, that all of them were a threat to her and her people. The two boys she had seen had looked harmless enough.

Mala had hurried back into the canyon after the boys had seen her. It wasn't until she had gotten to her ledge that she began to worry.

"The Other knows things," her mother and others had told her time and time again.

Mala believed that her people grossly overestimated the powers of The Other, or at least she had until she made her way from the ledge to the cave that she shared with her mother, and then she didn't know what to think. Mala had just rounded the shrubs bordering her ledge that had somehow managed to take root on the canyon wall when she saw him. She had sat on that ledge for quite some time before heading towards her cave, and had convinced herself that there was no need to report the sighting. Then there he was, she had almost ran right into him. The Other. As she had stood there face to face with him she hadn't known what to do. Silently she had stared, not knowing what to say, or even what to think, but the look he had given back to her had made her feel extremely uncomfortable. Her people had never been in the habit of wearing many clothes in the warmer months of the year. Mala had never had a second thought about being virtually unclad, but tonight for the first time in her life she had felt naked. She had almost been able to physically feel The Other's eyes upon her. As he looked closely up and down her slender, developing body with his hollow eyes, the expression he wore was unmistakable -- lust.

Not a single word had been exchanged between the two. After visually devouring her for what had seemed to Mala an eternity, The Other held his left index finger and pointed to his left eye, then he pointed his finger at her, as if to put an exclamation mark on the fact that he had seen her. Then under his wild mass of filthy, black hair he grinned at her lasciviously. Mala watched as he then turned and walked away, disappearing into the night.

Did he know that she had been seen by outsiders? Mala wondered. *If he did know, then why hadn't she been put in a cage. That had always been the fate of others who were guilty of serious crimes. They were kept in cages until it was time for their punishment to be carried out and it was time for the next feast.*

Mala also remembered something else her mother had warned her about The Other.

"You must never let him see you. If he sees you he's going to want to take you as a bride."

This possibility frightened Mala more than what the consequences could be for foolishly letting herself being sighted by an outsider.

Well he's seen me now, Mala thought, but she also knew that she had three more years before her sixteenth birthday when she would be eligible to marry. *If I'm careful not to let him see me again maybe he'll forget.*

She could fool herself into holding on to this hope, but deep down inside, Mala knew that The Outsider wasn't one to forget anything.

18.

It felt to Denny as though he had just closed his eyes when his father nudged him awake. It was light out now and everyone was awake.

"C'mon Denny, up you get. Were you two planning to sleep all day long?" Asked Mike.

Denny could see Shawn near by and by the look of him, Denny knew that his bother had just awakened as well. All of the strangeness of the previous night flooded back into his mind and he looked around for Lester and Johnny. He found them sitting a little ways away from everyone else as usual. They were sitting on a log together looking none the worse for wear after spending the night prowling around in the wilderness.

It occurred to Denny then that the Sabina twins never looked any the worse for wear. He couldn't remember either of them ever being sick. A cold or flu could make it's way through the entire student body of Vollmer's Hollow Public School and those two wouldn't get it. He couldn't remember either of them ever looking tired, or having the sniffles, or even sneezing. Except for a change in clothes they always looked exactly as they had the day before. He couldn't even remember them looking like they were in need of a hair cut.

Fuck those two are weird, he thought for the umpteenth time, and the longer he thought about them, the stranger they seemed.

After the boys had ate a quick breakfast, and had gathered their tents and other camping gear away into their backpacks they were on their way. Today the scout troop was going to go back to the camp site where they had spent their first night, and tomorrow they would make it back to the loop from where they would get back into their cars and mini vans and go home.

Denny and Shawn were both very tired from lack of sleep. They plodded along side by side for a long time, neither of them felt much like talking. They lagged behind most of the pack with only Lester and Johnny behind them. Finally the Jackson brothers got around to speaking.

"I wonder how long they were wandering around out there last night," said Denny nodding his head backwards towards the twins.

"Who knows," answered Shawn.

"Do you think they were in their sleeping bags when we got back?"

"I don't know," said Shawn. "I really couldn't tell from where we were." He took a few more paces and then added, "but I really don't think they made it back until after we were asleep."

"I wonder what they were doing out there," said Denny. "Do you think they saw Jake too?"

"Your guess is as good as mine, but I do think that they were following that big shit hawk," answered Shawn.

"Do you think that they knew we were following them?"

Shawn paused for a moment. He didn't understand why, but just as he had felt then, he didn't like the idea of the twins knowing that him and Denny had been following them.

"I don't know," he said finally, "but I wouldn't want to bet against it. I think those two know about a lot of things that no one thinks they do."

The Jackson brothers walked in silence for most of the rest of the day, but both knew that they were being

84

watched without having to turn around to look back at the twins. It made both Shawn and Denny feel very uneasy, and after all of the weirdness from the night before they were both more than ready to get back home to familiar surroundings without the added unrest that Lester and Johnny were now giving them.

By the time the scout troupe made it to the camp site it was early evening. Clouds had begun to roll in just before they stopped for lunch and had continued to build up throughout the day. This time when the scout leader told them to put up their tents before supper none of the boys complained. They had just finished another meal of beans and wieners when the first flash of lightning hit the sky. The lightning was quickly followed by a loud clap of thunder and a few minutes later the rain came.

Each of the tents had been designated to two boys. Shawn and Denny were paired up in one, and when the sky opened to let loose a downpour they scurried into it to avoid getting drenched. The wind picked up and the rain came down in sheets, but their little tent held fast.

With nothing separating them from Mother Nature's little temper tantrum but a thin sheet of nylon the boys felt very exposed. The thunder sounded louder to them now than it would have if they were at home with a sound roof over their heads, and every bolt of lightning appeared as though it were mere feet away.

Shawn and Denny began to feel cold and they both crawled into the warmth of their sleeping bags. They were exhausted from too little sleep and the day's long hike, and in spite of all the racket outside, and even though it was still only early evening, they both found slumber soon after.

Denny was plagued by disturbing dreams that night. In his sleep he again saw Jake Vollmer. He tried to look

85

only at Jake's good eye, but he was unable to help himself from gazing into the left side of his face and the dark, empty socket.

"You're not supposed to be here," he again heard Jake say with that look of panic and confusion on his face.

Then hundreds of red ants began boiling out of the black hole were his eye should have been. Denny recoiled and Jake began to laugh.

"How do you like that lad?" He asked.

Denny said nothing, but whatever expression he wore on his face caused Jake to tilt his head back and laugh harder still.

"Please leave me alone," Denny pleaded.

Jake stopped laughing abruptly. His amusement had quickly changed to anger.

"It's still my time!" He growled. "It's not your turn yet. You stay the hell away. Do you hear?"

Then the dream changed quickly and Denny saw the girl hiding in the tall grass. She stood up and he saw that she was naked except for the loin cloth just as he had seen her the night before.

Without saying a word she came to him. She put her hands on his shoulders and pressed herself close against him. Denny could feel her developing breasts on his chest. He had never stood like this with a girl before, and certainly not a nude one. His body was surging with electricity, his penis so hard it was aching. He put his hands on her hips and looked into her deep, brown eyes and lost himself totally in them. She leaned her face forward and gently brushed her lips against his. Then she took a hold of his right hand and guided it to her breast.

Denny awoke with a gasp. He had never had such a dream before. It had all seemed so real. He'd heard of wet dreams before of course, but had yet to experience one. He was still just a little too young to reach a true climax, but he now understood what it was the older boys he had overheard from time to time found so amazing about girls. Denny had already had many crushes and he knew what sex was, but before now he had never had any overwhelming desire to participate in the act.

In the next instant Denny became aware of sounds coming from two sources. He could hear Shawn stirring beside him, and he could hear quiet giggling coming from inside the tent at his feet.

The storm had passed, but only recently. Flashes of lightning in the distance still illuminated the night at the campsite. As Denny raised his head, one of these flashes revealed two platinum blonde heads. It was either Lester, Johnny, or both that had been giggling. That in itself was unusual. Try as he might, Denny couldn't remember either of them even coming close to laughing before.

They know about my dream, he thought. *They were inside my head while I was sleeping and they know all about it.*

Denny felt around by his side for the flashlight he had left there and when he found it he shone the beam on them.

"What are you guys doing in here?" He heard Shawn ask in a voice that betrayed a hint of fear.

It was then that Denny realized that Lester was chewing on something. Whatever it was it was hard and it was making clicking sounds against his teeth.

Both Shawn and Denny watched him for a moment puzzled. Then Lester put his hand to his mouth and took something out if it. He held an object out to them between his thumb and forefinger. Denny let the beam from the

87

flashlight rest on it and he saw it sparkle brightly -- gold. It was a gold nugget. Denny was sure of it.

Lester handed the nugget over to Johnny who in turn popped it into his mouth and swallowed. He stuck out his tongue and wagged it at Denny and Shawn to show that it was truly gone.

"You guys found the mine didn't you?" Asked Shawn.

The twins didn't answer. They turned from the Jackson brothers and exited the little tent. First Johnny, and then Lester.

When all had been silent for a few moments, Shawn turned to Denny.

"Did you see that?" Those two freakazoids found Jake's mine."

"I doubt it," said Denny.

"How can you doubt it? Where else could they have gotten the gold?"

"They probably just spray painted a stone," answered Denny. "I bet they had it before the hike even started."

"That wasn't any spray painted stone," insisted Shawn. "That was gold and you know it."

And in spite of what Denny had just said, he did know it.

Both Denny and Shawn's minds were now geared into overdrive and no matter how hard they tried, neither of them could get back to sleep. Denny's thoughts lingered on the beautiful young girl he had seen the night before and of the dream he'd just had of her. He thought about Jake Vollmer, and he thought about gold.

Had Lester and Johnny found the mine?

Shawn's mind was equally filled. He was certain that Jake's gold mine wasn't far from where they had seen his ghost.

How far from that boulder had Lester and Johnny gone to find it?

That night Shawn vowed that one day he would find it too. Then he wondered , *will the twins tell anyone about it?* He doubted it, but he didn't doubt that they would one day go back as well. *They are nuts, but they're not crazy enough just to forget about a mine full of gold. No one is that batty.*

As tired as Denny and Shawn had been the day before, yet another night of inadequate sleep had left them feeling much worse today. Today they plodded along so slowly that even the Sabina twins were ahead of them. This left the Jackson brothers a view of the back of their platinum blonde heads for the duration of the day. Shawn and Denny talked sporadically.

"We should come back out here by ourselves," said Shawn. "If those two could find the mine we can too."

The idea of trekking out here again, but this time alone with Shawn wasn't very appealing to Denny. Day time wouldn't be so bad, but when night fell ... . No he didn't like that idea at all. Especially with all the spooky shit that went on out here. Besides, their parents would never let them come out here alone anyway.

"Maybe we could ask Dad to come with us," said Denny. "We could tell him everything."

"Ya, like he's going to believe us," said Shawn.

"It wouldn't hurt to try."

"Then you go right ahead and tell him."

Denny had to grin. His brother was right, but Denny was also as sure as shit that he wasn't going to come out here alone with Shawn.

They walked in silence for a while longer and then they saw Johnny veer off the path to the right. He stood next to a large tree at an angle that kept him hidden from everyone ahead of him, but in clear view of Denny and Shawn. Then he hiked down his pants and squatted.

"Johnny's taking a shit," said Denny in amusement. "Or is that Lester?"

"It's Johnny," answered Shawn.

Johnny was quick about it, so quick in fact that Denny and Shawn had a hard time believing that he'd had enough time to take care of his business. He had his pants back up and was catching back up with Lester in no time.

"Do you think it's in there?" Asked Denny.

"Think what's in where?" Said Shawn not knowing what the hell his kid brother was talking about.

"The gold," said Denny. "Do you think it's in his shit?"

Now understanding, Shawn chuckled. "What if it is? Are you going to pick it out?"

"We could wrap it up in some leaves or something and wash it off later," said Denny.

"I'm not going to touch it."

"C'mon, let's just take a look."

Denny and Shawn went to the tree.

"It doesn't look like anything but a pile of shit to me," said Shawn when they got there.

Denny found this funny and began to laugh. He was also at that point of tiredness when things that would usually only seem mildly amusing to him were now hysterical and he fell into a fit of giggles.

90

"Let's get a stick," he said with his eyes watery from laughing.

"What the hell for?" Asked Shawn. He knew full well why Denny wanted a stick, but he wanted to hear Denny explain.

"So we can dig for gold," answered Denny.

Denny's reply had both boys laughing loudly while they looked for a stick. Shawn found one near by and he handed it over to Denny. "You have the honors," he said.

Denny took the stick and began poking Johnny's crap with it. He spread the little pile around and poked through it thoroughly, but he didn't find any gold. Just as he gave up, the boys heard an unexpected voice -- their father's. Neither of them had noticed Mike doubling back to check on them.

"What are you two doing?" He asked in a concerned tone.

Still with a stick in Johnny's shit Denny knew that he'd been caught red-handed and he didn't know what to say.

"Why are you doing that?" Asked Mike, his nose wrinkled in disapproval.

"Um, ... something to do," answered Denny.

"I'm sure that you can find something better to do," said Mike, but he was smiling. He still remembered well enough what it was like to be a boy, and he knew that sometimes boys did some really gross things for no apparent reason. "You guys have been lagging way behind all day. Are you feeling OK?"

"Just a little tired," answered Shawn.

"Is that helping to wake you up?" Asked Mike looking down at the little pile.

Neither of the boys said anything and Denny, who was still holding the stick, could only look up at his father with a sheepish grin.

"Well c'mon," said Mike. "Put that stick down and try to keep up. We haven't got too much farther left to go now."

19.

Everything that they had experienced during that hike stayed with Denny and Shawn. For the first few days after they got home they talked about it a lot.

The Jackson brothers shared bunk beds. Being the oldest, Shawn had gotten first choice of upper and lower, and he had chosen the upper. For more than a week after their adventure when the boys retired each night, Shawn would rest his head by the edge of the bed and talk to Denny about his plan to one day return to the area where they had seen Jake Vollmer and find the gold mine. Each night it was almost exactly the same conversation, but neither of them tired of talking about it, or of dreaming about the riches of the secret gold mine.

"Shawn, what do you think he meant by saying that it wasn't our turn yet?" Denny had asked one night.

"I don't know. Maybe Jake doesn't even know he's dead."

Denny had always been fascinated by the paranormal. Residents of Vollmer's Hollow had long been aware that television reception in their neck of the woods left much to be desired. So far no cable company had deemed it profitable enough to run a line all the way from Tamarack to the little town, and only the fortunate few had bothered with satellite. The Jacksons however, were one of those fortunate few. There were channels on satellite that often aired programming about a variety of paranormal phenomenon including ghosts and hauntings. Denny watched these shows every chance he got and he read a lot of books on such dark subjects as well.

As in any town or city in probably every country in the world, Vollmer's Hollow had it's fair share of ghost

93

stories. There were houses in the little community that many of the children (and more than a few adults) had become convinced were haunted. There was a boarding house on St. George St. that had been deemed by many of these children to be the most haunted house in town, and given the history of the place it wasn't hard to see why. The house had once been used as a sort of nursing home. It had been run by a disturbed woman and it had been discovered after quite a period of time that this woman had been killing many of the patients there. It was also rumored that she had killed both of her daughters, although that had never been conclusively proven.

If the boarding house was the champion haunted house of Vollmer's Hollow the number one contender was a house that had once been a mortuary. Once upon a time the mortician who had lived there had hung himself in a closet on the second story of the house. This house was now a duplex and it had long been the setting for all sorts of tales about strange goings on.

As Denny learned more about the town's history, he became more and more convinced that Vollmer's Hollow didn't merely have it's fair share of skeletons in it's closet, it had an overwhelming surplus of them.

Time distances events, and for a pair of young boys in the midst of summer holidays it only required a short period of time for Shawn and Denny Jackson to distance themselves from the things they had experienced during their hike with the boy scouts. The two would never forget the night they had met Jake Vollmer, nor would they ever forget about his gold mine, but for now it wasn't often one of the foremost thoughts in their minds.

Even though Mike had decided that perhaps Wade wasn't such as bad a guy as he had initially thought he did keep to his decision not to force his sons to attend any further boy scout meetings or outings. If they decided on their own that they wanted to go that would be fine with him, but as the summer vacation wore on, neither Shawn or Denny had mentioned anything about wanting to participate in any further scout activities. Instead both signed up for summer baseball and spent much of their additional spare time fishing in front of an old shanty and hanging out with their friends.

Shawn and Denny were informed by Bobby and Carl that the Sabina twins had also dropped out of scouts. As a matter of fact, no one had seen them around anywhere. Even though Lester and Johnny were far from popular, they were notable, and many of the younger residents of Vollmer's Hollow found it odd that they never saw the twins again for the entire summer. After the two months of summer vacation were over they also found that the two were no longer attending school.

"They must have moved away," Bobby reasoned, and that was a good enough explanation for their disappearance for everyone.

Now that they were back into a regular routine and most of their days were filled with their studies at school, Denny all but completely forgot about the things they had seen in the canyon. It wasn't long before Lester and Johnny Sabina became distant memories as well.

20

Vollmer's Hollow High School is very small when compared with most others in the country, but to Denny Jackson it seemed enormous when he entered it for the first time as a student. He had been in the building several times before for various reasons. The gymnasium often served as a community hall.

In public school most of his classes had been carried out in a single room. When one class ended he simply lifted the lid on his desk and replaced one text book for another. In high school however, everyone was assigned a locker and each class was held in a different room. As he went to his locker for the first time after a morning orientation, Denny felt that this was a major step on his road to adulthood. *First your own locker, then your own car, then your own home.*

Denny was happy to find that his two closest elementary buds, Bobby and Carl, had their lockers on either side of his. It was good to have familiar faces around in unfamiliar surroundings. Actually, all of the faces in all of his classes save for those of a couple of the newer teachers were familiar. Most of the faces in the entire town were familiar in the little community for that matter.

The youngest Mr. Jackson, Bobby, and Carl also shared the same home room. Since there was only two home rooms for freshmen students, the chances of that happening really hadn't been all that astounding. All three teens were also going to be in the same first class of the day together, English.

Onward to the wonderful world of high school English, Denny thought. He remembered seeing the same text book for the class a year earlier when Shawn began high school. Denny remembered thinking how much more sophisticated Shawn's text had looked compared to the one's used in the public school. A year still seemed like an eternity to a thirteen year old, but at long last, here he was.

As the three made their way up the stairs in search of room 201, Denny's vision of self maturity was quickly shattered when a group of seniors passed them on their way down.

"Where's your beanies you little turds?" Asked Troy Hines. Then he turned to his buddies and laughed loudly as though he had just created the wittiest joke on earth.

Troy was easy for the boys to recognize. He was the captain of the football team and one of the most popular boys in school in spite of what in Denny's mind was a rather repulsive personality. As Denny's mother would say, he was just a little too full of himself.

Troy's cronies laughed along with him even though they'd already heard the same joke twice that morning. This group of senior students didn't harass Denny and company any further, but it had been a quick reminder to them that the next day initiation week began.

"I'd almost forgotten about the beanies," said Carl.

All of the grade nine students would have to make sure that they wore beanies for the duration of the week lest they were hauled off to kangaroo court to suffer severe consequences.

"They can't really do anything to us if we don't wear them, can they?" Asked Bobby.

"I'm not going to get caught without one," said Denny.

"Pussy," said Bobby. "I'm not wearing one."

97

Bobby of the flaming red hair who had always been a tough little kid had gone through a growth spurt over the summer. Denny didn't doubt that he wasn't afraid of any of the seniors in high school including Troy Hines.

"Did you hear what they did to Matt Hagen two years ago?" Asked Denny.

"What?" Said Bobby.

"They made him eat marshmallows."

"I like marshmallows," cut in Carl.

"Yeah, but a bunch of the seniors made a line up and he had to chew them out from their armpits," said Denny.

"Gross!" Said Carl.

"They can't make you do stuff like that," said Bobby. "All they can make you do is carry their books or wash floors with a toothbrush and stuff like that."

"Maybe," said Denny, "but I'm not taking any chances. Besides, who's going to care. All of the other grade niners are going to have to wear beanies, and all of the older kids had to wear them when they were in grade nine too. It's not like we're going to be the only ones."

Bobby had no further argument on the subject. He really didn't care that he had to wear a beanie, and he could take a few insults thrown his way from the likes of Troy Hines, but if they tried to do anything that he felt was uncalled for, look out.

Denny, Bobby, and Carl had thought that they had been fairly quick about getting to their first class, but as they entered the room they discovered that they were probably the last ones to arrive. They had planned to sit near each other, but the teacher told them to quickly pick a desk. Carl and Bobby ended up on one side of the room and Denny, who didn't see any available seats near them spotted one on the other side of the room and hastily took it.

Almost immediately after they sat, the teacher gave them his name and began to tell the class about what material he had scheduled to go over with them over the course of the year. Denny found it quite humorous that his English teacher's name was Mr. French.

It didn't take Denny long to realize that none of what Mr. French was talking about today was anything that he was going to see on a test, it was merely an overview of what they were going to cover. Denny shut out his teacher's monotone and he began to scan the back of the heads of his fellow classmates who were sitting in front of him. He could tell who all of them were even from this view. Then his eyes settled on a long, raven mane with a little white ribbon tied in it. Denny's heart jumped. He was immediately reminded of the girl he had seen hiding in the tall grass just a little over a year earlier. He stared at the girl for a long time and convinced himself that this had to be that very same girl. When she finally turned her head enough for him to see her face however, he saw that although her features were very close to those of that Indian girl with the little white flowers in her hair, she wasn't that girl, and judging by her fair complexion she wasn't of Indian descent. She was a looker though. *Almost as pretty as the canyon girl,* Denny told himself. He had never seen her before, so he knew that she must have only recently moved to Vollmer's Hollow.

Even after he had realized that this was someone other than who he had first thought she was, Denny couldn't keep himself from staring at her. Mr. French turned his back from the class to write on the board and something wet hit the side of Denny's face -- a spit ball.

He looked into the direction of where it had come from and he found Bobby looking at him. Bobby was holding his hand over his mouth and was bouncing up and down pretending that he had an uncontrollable case of the snickers. Then he held his hands up near his eyes as though he were holding binoculars and pretended to zoom in on the girl that Denny had been looking at. Then Bobby looked back over at Denny and rubbed his two fore fingers together in a tsk tsk gesture.

Denny couldn't help but smile back. He'd been caught gawking at a pretty girl and now his good buddy was going to razz him a little about it.

Then Denny saw that Bobby was looking at whomever it was that was sitting behind him. Then he looked back at the girl Denny had been staring at, and then behind Denny again. He repeated this again a couple more times and Denny knew that Bobby wanted him to take a look at the person that was sitting behind him. Denny had been in such a hurry to find a seat when he had entered the room that he hadn't paid any attention to any of the other students in his class including the one sitting at his rear.

Mr. French returned his attention to the class and Bobby quit his miming, but now Denny desperately wanted to take a peek at his back yard neighbor. From the way that Bobby had been carrying on, Denny was pretty sure that it was a girl -- either an especially ugly one, or another pretty one who was sitting behind him. He was a little nervous about turning around and openly gaping at her, especially if she was a babe. That would hardly be the correct thing to do. He was just going to have to wait until the English class was over before he could have a look.

Even though all of today's classes were abbreviated because of a morning assembly to welcome all of the students of Vollmer's Hollow High to another school year, today's English class seemed to Denny to drag on forever.

Finally when the bell rang and his classmates began to collect their books in preparation to move on to whichever room they had their next class in, Denny turned sideways in his seat and looked behind him. He saw that it was indeed a girl back there and that she too was pretty just like the girl that he had been staring at. As a matter of fact, she looked exactly like that other girl. She looked at Denny and smiled.

"Hello, I'm Nicole," she said holding out her hand.

"I'm Denny," he said taking the hand that she offered while taking note of her sparkling, green eyes.

"This is my sister Candace," said Nicole as she looked up past Denny.

Denny turned and saw Candace standing by looking down at him. Then he looked back at Nicole. *Babes in stereo*, he thought, and then he looked back at Candace. They had to be identical twins. Denny was reminded of Lester and Johnny, the only other identical twins he had ever known.

As if reading his mind, Candace spoke up, "Yeah, we're twins." Then both girls began giggling.

Denny immediately loved the sound of their laughter which was also identical to one another, and the two sets of dancing green eyes looking at him made him feel good all over. Denny was smitten. The only trouble was he didn't know which of the girls he was more taken with. They were so much the same, that to be attracted to either one of them was to be attracted to both.

Nicole finished collecting her books before Denny even started to pick up his. His mind was lost totally on his two new acquaintances. He wanted to talk to them some

101

more, but he had no idea what to say. Candace rescued him from the awkward moment.

"What do you have next?" She asked.

"History," answered Denny.

"So do we," said Nicole.

"See you there," said Candace, and then her and Nicole were off chattering and giggling along the way.

Denny hurriedly picked up his books. He wanted to get a seat next to those twins in history. He had only made it to the back of his aisle of desks when some of his books slipped out from the stack he was carrying under his arm and fell noisily to the floor.

"How's that going klutz?" He heard Bobby's voice say. "You've been hanging around with Carl too much.

"Hah, hah! Very funny," said Carl.

Candace and Nicole had made Denny forget all about Bobby and Carl.

"I see that you got your tongue back up off the floor," said Bobby.

Denny blushed, "what do you mean?" He said, feigning ignorance.

"You know what I mean, you were just a drooling at that chick up there."

"Denny's in love, Denny's in love," chanted Carl.

"That had to be her twin sister that was sitting there behind you too," said Bobby. "They are pretty hot aren't they?"

"Do you think they eat bugs like Lester and Johnny did?" Asked Carl.

Denny rolled his eyes up towards the ceiling and Bobby quit talking for a moment. Then they both called out in unison," butt wipe!" And each punched Carl in a

102

shoulder. That was the punishment the three of them had devised in grade eight for saying something lame.

Bobby and Carl both had math for their next class, so when they got outside the door of the English room the three parted ways and Denny headed for the history room. When he got there he again found that he was probably the last to get there, he quickly scanned the room and found Candace with Nicole sitting at the desk directly behind her. The seat to the right of Candace was empty so Denny plopped himself into that one.

Mr. Pearce, the history teacher, was momentarily preoccupied with some paperwork at his desk and it gave the students a chance to talk with each other.

"I haven't seen you two around before," said Denny.

"We just moved here about a week ago," said Candace.

Denny was encouraged by this. He had known that they were new to Vollmer's Hollow, but he'd figured that they had probably moved a month or two ago. A week was really new, and it meant that they probably hadn't had enough time to meet very many people, -- particularly boys.

Before history class ended, Denny had found that Candace had had enough time to meet a guy after all. His name was Brent and he lived next door to her. When Candace and Nicole's family were moving in to their new place Brent had come over and given them a hand. Denny knew Brent and where he lived, so now he also knew where the twins lived. He also found out that Nicole was still unattached, and when lunch break rolled around he found himself sitting with her in the cafeteria.

Bobby and Carl had sought Denny out at lunch, but when they saw that their buddy and Nicole seemed to be hitting it off so well together they thought it better not to interrupt them.

"Lookie that," said Bobby. "Our first day of high school and Denny already has a girlfriend."

The three hadn't talked about it much, but Bobby, Carl, and Denny had known when they graduated elementary school, that at some point over the course of their time in high school at least one of them, if not all, would eventually find a girlfriend. They all felt that they were going to be friends forever, but they knew that when relationships with females began to enter into the picture their friendship wouldn't be quite the same. Bobby hadn't expected it to happen so fast.

"Let's go razz him," said Carl.

"No," said Bobby, "let's just leave them alone. It figures he'd be the first of us to get a chick anyway.

"Why's that?" Asked Carl.

"'Cause me and you are ugly fuckers."

"Ugh?"

"You heard me."

"What do you mean?"

"Well," said Bobby, "my bright red head probably glows in the dark, and you look like Barney after a pudding eating binge."

"Butt wipe," said Carl with a confused look on his face, and he punched Bobby in the shoulder half-heartedly.

From that first lunch together on, Denny and Nicole spent as much time together as possible. Before long everyone they knew found it odd to see one without the other somewhere near by.

Candace's relationship with the boy next door hadn't lasted long and she went through a handful of other boyfriends over the period of time that her sister had been with Denny. She even dated Shawn a few times, and although they liked each other as friends they never found that mysterious chemistry like Denny and Nicole had.

Although Candace was happy for Nicole and wished her no ill will, she was secretly envious of her sister. She had a crush on Denny that she never told anyone about and as the school year began when she entered the eleventh grade, she remembered that first day her and Nicole had met Denny. Candace knew that back then, it could have been her just as easily as Nicole to have been the one sitting with the dashing, young Mr. Jackson in the cafeteria. It was funny how things worked out sometimes.

21.

Although Denny spent the vast majority of his free time with Nicole, he never forgot about his friends. Bobby had continued to grow and was now half a head taller than Carl and a full head taller than Denny. He had also filled out and had become the strongest student in Vollmer's Hollow High. Bobby also still had that temper that at times could approach raging. He'd had three fights in grade ten and had won them all so easily that word got out that he wasn't one to be messed with and he hadn't had another one since.

Carl had grown as well, but unfortunately for him, so had his girth and clumsiness. If it hadn't been for his close friendship with Bobby, Carl would most likely have found himself on the wrong end of a lot of jokes.

As they reached the mid term of their eleventh grade, Denny, Bobby, and Carl all knew that the time was drawing near for them to be doing some serious planning on what they were going to do with the rest of their lives.

A college scout had caught wind of Bobby's abilities on the football field and had taken the trip to the Hollow to see him play. Bobby had scored four touchdowns in that game and sacked the opposing quarterback three times thus salting away a scholarship for himself. Carl hadn't decided what he wanted to do after high school yet, but Bobby and Denny both knew that he would probably wind up with a mindless job in Vollmer's Hollow. They also knew that in all likelihood he'd be happy with this job and would probably live out his entire life right there in the little town they had all grown up in.

As for Denny, he had gained an interest in something that had surprised both Bobby and Carl, -- accounting. Denny's friends had tried to sway him into pursuing some sort of career that would involve writing for they both had enjoyed a lot of his tall tales over the years.

"You've always been so good at making up stories," Bobby told him. "It would be a waste to throw that away."

"Maybe I'll do some writing on the side," Denny had told him. "Besides, other than the mechanics of writing, I don't think that there are any courses that can teach you how to write. Either you've got an aptitude for it or you don't, it's as simple as that. They can't teach you imagination, so I don't think that there really is any course I could enroll in even if I wanted to. I'll be taking some English while I'm studying accounting though, I'm sure there will be some writing in that."

Bobby and Carl accepted what Denny had told them and they thought it better not to push the issue. True friends didn't harass each other on such matters. Besides, although it sounded awfully boring to them, accounting was just as good a career as any.

Denny had also been talking about the future with Nicole. Marriage had been discussed on more than one occasion, and even though Nicole's parents didn't particularly approve of her getting into such a serious relationship at such a young age, both her and Denny couldn't imagine really being happy if they weren't together, and although they didn't have their life's plan carved into stone, Denny and Nicole were pretty sure that Denny would go on to become an accountant, and Nicole a nurse. Then the two would get married, move to Tamarack or some place like that where the world offered more opportunities than a backwards little place like Vollmer's Hollow, and live happily ever after.

A lifetime is filled with many unexpected twists and turns however, and Denny and Nicole were about to discover a big one in their road.

22.

Nicole's father was a ship builder. As the only port on Lake Sasquatch, Vollmer's Hollow's fishing fleet was a fairly large one, and a contract for building fishing tugs had been the reason Mr. MacDonald had brought his family to the sleepy little town in the first place.

An uncle of his in Seattle had been trying to lure Mr. MacDonald to his ship yard for years. Bernard MacDonald however, had felt that to work for an uncle would be like going for a free ride and he would never know if he was really any good at his craft or was merely being patronized because of being the nephew of a man who was in a position to grant him instant success.

As the years went by however, Bernard gained confidence by receiving acclaim from people who had no idea of his blood ties to the Seattle ship building tycoon and he longed for the challenge of building ships that would see the vast waters of the ocean.

"We're moving to Seattle," he announced one evening at the dinner table.

His wife, who hadn't cared much for the move to the Hollow in the first place was quite pleased, and Candace was somewhat indifferent. Nicole on the other hand was stunned. She immediately excused herself from the table and went to her room where she cried for a long time.

This can't be happening, she thought. *I can't leave Denny.*

She thought about talking to her parents to see if they would let her stay behind, but she knew that her father would find the idea preposterous. He thought of her and

109

Denny's relationship as nothing more than puppy love. She had heard him use that exact term in the past when he had tried to convince her that her and Denny were spending far too much time together.

"Sweetheart, you're far too young to be seeing only one person. You're only going to be young once and you should be dating other boys, it's the only way that you're going to find the one that you are going to be truly happy with."

"But I love Denny," Nicole had replied, "and there's no one that I'd be happier with."

"I know that you think you love him," said Bernard, "but it's only puppy love, and in a few short years you're going to realize that."

Nicole hadn't argued, but she had been furious with her father.

He doesn't know how I feel. She had thought. *How could he? I'm not too young to be in love. I'm almost seventeen. That's pretty much grown up. It's about time Dad quit treating me like I was a child.*

It had been much easier to let the matter drop than to try to convince him to understand her point of view however, after all, they weren't forbidding her from seeing Denny, and she knew that they liked him. They were merely trying to tell her that they didn't think that she should be limiting herself to dating only one person.

Now Nicole wondered if it might not have been better for her to have stood her ground. Possibly she could have made her parents understand how she felt. Now it was too late. Bernard MacDonald was strict with his daughters, there was no way he would leave one of them behind, and Nicole was going to have to move to Seattle whether she liked it or not.

110

When she got herself pulled together, Nicole decided to call Denny. *Maybe he'll know what to do.*

"Hello?" It was Shawn who answered.

"Hi Shawn, could I speak to Denny please?"

Shawn noticed that Nicole hardly sounded like her usual happy self. Thinking something was wrong he said, "just a sec," and hollered for his brother. After a short moment Denny was on the line.

"We need to talk," Nicole told him.

"Is everything okay?"

"That's what we need to talk about. I'll come over to your house."

"Okay," said Denny. *What's going on?* He wondered. *She sounds so sad, maybe she's going to dump me.* "I'll start walking and meet you half way."

Denny and Nicole often met this way after one had called the other. More often than not when they got face to face they found themselves in front of a little park on St. George St. The park had a rusty, old swing set that the two would swing on side by side as they chatted away, sometimes for considerably long periods of time. Tonight when they met, they kissed and headed for the swings as usual.

"What do we need to talk about?" Denny asked. "You sounded a little upset on the phone."

"We're moving," Nicole blurted. "To Seattle."

Denny looked just as shocked as he would have had she slapped him across the face. Nicole knew that he didn't know what to say. Seeing him sitting there in the swing beside her like so many times before reminded her that soon they wouldn't be able to do this anymore. She hadn't realized it until now, but these moments here in the park with Denny had grown very special to her. They were

111

perhaps a little too old to be playing on swing sets, but to her this was their special place. There was rarely anyone else in the little park and the two of them had spent so much time here alone doing nothing but enjoying each other's company that it seemed to her that it truly was theirs. All of this flashed through Nicole's mind quickly and before she knew it, fresh tears were streaming from her eyes.

When Denny finally managed to speak, it was only a single word he uttered that sounded more croaked than spoken. "When?"

"As soon as school lets out for the summer."

Denny's mind was spinning as the reality of what his girlfriend had just told him set in. *This can't be happening,* he thought. *It's not fair. Nicole can't go, she's the best thing that ever happened to me.* School was out in two weeks. Denny knew that those two weeks would pass like the blink of an eye. Then she would be gone and there was nothing he could do about it.

Neither Nicole or Denny said anything else for a long time. Denny reached over to wipe the tears from Nicole's cheek all the while battling furiously to hold on to his own. Finally he lost the battle.

"No," he muttered quietly and his chest began to hitch as he broke down. Nicole got out of her swing and went to him and the two clung to each other crying for what seemed a very long time.

23

When the bell sounded to end the final class of the school year Denny's heart sank. Normally he looked forward to summer vacation. For the last two years he had spent it almost entirely with Nicole. This year however, the beginning of summer holidays only meant that the time for her departure was here. She was leaving tomorrow.

Over the two weeks since they had learned that she was leaving, the two had spent every minute possible together. They had made plans to keep in touch via the internet. Denny told Nicole that he was pretty sure that he could get a job working in the kitchen at a restaurant called Spencer's on the beach in Vollmer's Hollow.

"I'll save every penny I can, and when I have enough money, I can come out to Seattle to see you."

Denny also knew that his parents were going to foot the bill for him to go to college when he graduated high school the next year. Shawn was already enrolled at the Tamarack university where he was going to take a graphic arts course.

"Maybe I can try to work it out so I can go to school in Seattle."

All of this talk was encouraging to the young couple. At sixteen a year still seemed like a very long time, but at least now they had hope that it was possible that they would one day be reunited.

The classes for the final day of school had been shortened to allow for an assembly that afternoon, but Denny and Nicole had decided to skip the assembly so they could spend her last day in the Hollow together. The two

113

wandered around town for a while hand in hand and then they went down to Spencer's for dinner.

Denny and Nicole hadn't yet had sex, but as they walked out of Spencer's Nicole whispered into Denny's ear. "I want to make love to you before I go."

As dusk began to turn to darkness, the two went to Denny's house where he snuck a blanket and then they headed for a secluded spot on the beach.

Once on the beach, Denny spread the blanket out on the sand and there the two kissed and touched one another for a long while before they timidly began removing their clothing, both knowing that this was the other's first time.

When they were finished the young lovers wrapped themselves into the blanket. Still naked and with no need for words, they laid where they were taking comfort in each other's warmth. Here they intended to remain until once again the sun lit up the sky.

"You'll probably get into trouble with your folks," Denny warned.

"I don't care," said Nicole.

Denny had been dozing when he was roused by a familiar sound. He wasn't as worried this time as he had been the first time he had heard it during the hike with the boy scouts that now seemed like so long ago.

"What's that?" Nicole whispered in a sleepy voice.

"I'll tell you in a minute," Denny whispered back and he held a forefinger over Nicole's soft lips.

The shit hawk was circling them the same way it had circled the camp during the hike, and the same as it had then, it's circle got tighter and tighter until it was flying directly over them. Finally it swooped low and let out one of it's ear piercing screeches causing Nicole to jump and clutch at Denny. Then the giant seagull flew away.

After it had been gone a short while Nicole again asked, "what was it?"

As Denny told her his tale the sky was just beginning to lighten, indicating that it would soon be time for them to go. It also allowed Denny to see Nicole's clouded expression as he talked and he could tell that although she wanted to believe him, she wasn't sure if she did or not.

"Why haven't you mentioned anything about it before?" She asked.

"Because I knew that it sounded crazy."

Denny didn't bother to tell her that falling in love with her had made him forget all about it.

24.

As he had hoped, Denny landed himself a job at Spencer's. He found that there was a lot more to restaurant work than he had suspected. In the past he had always figured that all there was to it was a bunch of people messing around in the kitchen ready to go home the minute the OPEN sign was turned off. What he found was that there was an awful lot more dishes and prep work to be done than he ever would have imagined, and when that was all done there was a huge mess to clean up at the end of the day as well.

Denny didn't mind his job, but his heart wasn't in it. His heart wasn't into anything these days. All he could think about was Nicole and how badly he missed her. There was a chat program on his family's computer and he talked to her with that and emailed her every day, but it just wasn't the same as seeing her sweet, smiling face and being able to reach out and touch her.

Shawn could see how down his kid brother was he and tried to cheer him up from time to time, but nothing seemed to work. He had even heard Denny trying to stifle sobs from behind the bathroom door on a couple of occasions. Denny's parents were also concerned, but they told Shawn that he would eventually snap out of it.

"It really is true that time has a way of healing all wounds," his mother had said.

Denny however, at least for the time being, didn't want to feel better. His reasoning was that for him to feel better would mean that he was over Nicole and he didn't want to be over her, not now, not ever.

Denny worked as many hours as he could get at Spencer's, almost all of them on afternoons. He quietly held in contempt a small number of the staff who he felt took this job way too seriously as far as he was concerned.

Some of these people really think that they're important, he thought It reminded him of a saying he heard his father use before, "if you take yourself too seriously, no one else has to."

All that mattered to Denny was the tally he kept in his head as each hour went by. *Another hour's pay closer to Nicole,* he thought to himself.

After a rare day shift about midway through summer vacation Shawn had some news for Denny.

"The twins are back."

Denny's heart jumped. *They're back? Nicole never mentioned anything about her and Candace coming ...*

Shawn saw the excited expression on his brother's face and chastised himself for not phrasing himself better. "Lester and Johnny are back, Kimmy told me this morning that she saw them yesterday when she was shopping with Mom"

Denny's heart settled back down. "Oh," he said, after a pause he added, "are you sure Kimmy saw them?" The boys' younger sister often liked to make things up.

"I think so," said Shawn. "When Kimmy is telling stories I can usually tell. I had forgotten all about Lester and Johnny, but do you know what hearing about them reminded me of?"

"Gross delicacies?" Denny managed in spite of the disappointment he felt that the twins Kimmy had been talking about were Lester and Johnny and not Nicole and Candace.

117

"Well, that too, but what it really reminded me of was the gold mine. Back then we were too young to go back to the canyon and look for it on our own, but we're old enough now."

Denny's most recent encounter with the giant shit hawk had reminded him of the mine, but his broken heart had quickly made him forget again. "Do you really think it's out there?" He asked.

"They say that legends usually begin with some sort of truth," Shawn said, "and with all of that other weird shit we saw going on out there how far fetched of an idea is a lost gold mine? It's a lot more believable than one-eyed ghosts and giant shit hawks."

"I suppose you have a point there," said Denny.

"So what do you think? Maybe we can get Bobby and Carl to go too."

Denny really didn't want to take any time off work. He knew that if they went to the canyon they'd be gone for at least four days. Those were days that he could be making money to put towards his planned trip to Seattle.

As if reading Denny's mind Shawn went on. "If there really is a gold mine, we'll be rich. We'll have enough money to do anything we want."

Denny hadn't thought about that. He had been too certain that Jake's mine was nothing more than a myth. *What if we do find some gold?* He thought. The rock that Lester and Johnny had shown them in the tent that night had sure looked like gold.

"Well?" Shawn asked.

"I don't know," said Denny. "Let me think about it."

"Well don't think too long, summer's going to be over before too much longer. When will you know?"

"Tomorrow," said Denny.

"All right, but try to let me know by morning okay?"

"Okay"

Later that evening Denny went out for a walk. He knew when he left the house where he was headed, but he got there in a roundabout way. He walked along Main Street and stopped to look in a couple of the store windows. The hardware store and it's fishing equipment set out on display was the only window that held his interest for any length of time. Then he headed for St. George St. and the little park, -- his and Nicole's little park.

He sat on the swing set and rocked gently back and forth. If he closed his eyes it was easy for him to imagine that Nicole was sitting in the swing next to him where she had always sat when the two of them used to come out here together. Missing of course was her happy chatter and the sound of her sweet laughter. A single tear escaped the corner of Denny's eye and tickled it's way down his cheek.

Stop it, he told himself. *You'll see her again one day and you're going to chat with her on the Internet in an hour.* Then he forced himself to think about other things.

Maybe trying to find the gold mine isn't such a bad idea after all. Denny thought about the girl that he had seen hiding in the tall grass the night Shawn and him had seen Jake's ghost. He had always known that both Nicole and Candace had reminded him a lot of her, and he still wondered what she had been doing out there. He remembered all the stories he had heard about the Sasquatch Indians and how some people liked to speculate that they were still out there somewhere in the wilderness between Vollmer's Hollow and Tamarack.

Maybe she's still out there, he thought. *Maybe she's a Sasquatch Indian.* She sure didn't look like any cannibal that he'd ever imagined though. Then he thought about the gold. *If it really is out there and we find it I could go to Seattle even before summer ends. If we found enough of it I could go out there whenever I wanted, maybe even move there and finish high school with Nicole.*

It was nice to dream.

By the time Denny got back home for his computer "date" he had made up his mind.

"Let's do it," he told Shawn.

Their father had overheard. "Do what?" He asked.

"We're going to go for another hike by the canyon," said Shawn.

Mike almost blurted that he thought that was a great idea and that they should make it a family affair, but then he caught himself. Shawn and Denny were old enough to go on their own (even though he knew their mother might be a little less convinced of that than he was) and if they had wanted their parents and Kimmy tagging along they would have asked them. Instead he said, "that sounds like a good idea."

With that it was settled. Shawn and Denny were going to go back to the canyon and look for Jake Vollmer's gold mine.

25.

It didn't take any persuasion at all for Denny to get
Carl and Bobby to come along for the adventure. Bobby
had recently bought a pickup truck that had long ago seen
better days. To him and the other boys however, it was the
greatest thing on wheels. They had decided that they
would all climb aboard the little ATVs that Shawn and
Denny's father had bought for them shortly after
dismantling the bike ramp once they got to the loop to
speed up progress to the canyon, and Bobby offered to use
his truck to get the ATVs and camping equipment to the
loop

Carl wasn't exactly keen on the idea of being out in
the wilderness once again, he would have preferred to stay
home with his video games, but he idolized Bobby and as
far as Carl was concerned, whatever Bobby was doing was
the thing to do.

That summer Bobby and Shawn had both been
working for the same lawn care business. Their boss had
been a little reluctant to let both of them have the same four
days off, but in the end he understood how much the boys
wanted to go, and he felt that he could make do for a little
while without them. Denny booked the days off from
Spencer's, and Carl who didn't have a summer job, was
free anyway, although he wasn't going to have much
money to chip in for supplies.

It was a Thursday morning when the boys were set
to head out. Bobby and his rusty old truck was at Shawn
and Denny's at eight AM. The plan was for them to pick
up Carl and drive out to the loop immediately afterward,
but when they got to Carl's house they found that he hadn't

even gotten out of bed yet. His mother whom looked remarkably like a pudgier version of her son answered the door wearing a flannel night gown that looked to be way too warm to be comfortable in at this time of the year, especially in the midst of a heat wave.

Delores' eyes were puffy with sleep and her hair was all askew.

"Sorry boys, Carl never has been much of a morning person," she said. "If you want to come on in I'll put on some coffee and wake him up."

Then Delores turned back into the house leaving the door open so the boys could follow. Shawn and Denny both grinned when they saw Bobby roll his eyes. They had all known that Carl was probably going to be a pain in the ass on this trip, but they hadn't expected him to start so early. In spite of his clumsiness and lazy nature however, Carl was just as much a part of the group as any of them, and they wouldn't think of leaving him behind.

As the boys sat in the kitchen waiting they could hear Delores' muffled voice as she tried to get Carl out of bed.

"Ah shit!" They clearly heard Carl say. "Eight O'clock already?"

Bobby, Shawn, and Denny couldn't help but snicker. They could hear Mrs. Montgomery's voice again, and they knew that she was scolding her son for his use of profanity.

Carl came stumbling into the kitchen soon after.

"My, but aren't you a sight first thing in the morning?" Said Bobby, then him and the Jackson's laughed. Carl looked so dopey that he almost seemed to be in pain as he poured himself a cup of coffee.

"You guys want some?"

Carl was the only one of the four boys who was an habitual coffee drinker, but as long as they had to wait anyway, the other three thought that they might as well join him.

"Okay, but hurry up," said Denny.

"I hope you're already packed," said Bobby. "We don't want to wait two hours for you to get ready."

"Yeah, I packed last night," answered Carl as he handed steaming mugs to his friends. "I won't be long, I just have to get dressed.

"No shower?" Asked Denny.

"I showered last night."

"Well you didn't get all of that ugly washed off," said Bobby.

"Ha ha, very funny!" Already Carl was beginning to revive to his normal level of dopiness.

It usually took about an hour to drive to the loop, but today it took the group of boys twenty minutes longer than that. Bobby drove more slowly than usual. His tail gate sometimes opened on it's own, and he didn't want to take any unnecessary chances on having that happen and allowing one or both of the ATVs to spill out onto the road.

"How did you ever get this thing through the safety check?" Carl had asked.

They had also had to stop twice to let Carl take a leak. He had quickly drank two cups of coffee in his kitchen and had drank another on the way, and now it all wanted back out.

When they finally got to the loop it was a quarter past ten and it was already hot. By mid-afternoon the day was going to be a real scorcher. The heat wave they were in had already lasted four days and wasn't showing any signs of letting up.

"Well, here we are," said Bobby. "Four stooges looking for a lost gold mine."

"That's us," agreed Denny.

Shawn and Denny had never told Bobby or Carl about seeing Jake's ghost, or that because of seeing him they had a stronger belief than the other two that the mine actually existed. They had been reluctant to talk about it because Bobby could be relentless at razzing someone, especially when he suspected someone was feeding him bullshit and expecting him to believe it.

The boys had driven with the windows down and the breeze that had been blowing in on them had made the day seem a lot cooler than it really was. Now that they had stopped, the cab of the truck was quickly becoming stifling, especially with all four of them crammed into it.

"Are we going to sit in here all day?" Asked Carl who was already sweating profusely.

They piled out of the truck and went to the back of it. Bobby gave the tail gate a yank and was surprised when it didn't easily fall open. He yanked again harder and still it wouldn't open.

"Figures," he said. "Fucking thing won't stay shut most of the time, and then when you want it to open ..."

Slightly annoyed he reefed on the tail gate with a little more force. It gave away this time -- completely. Bobby had yanked it right off of the truck, and he fell on his ass while still holding onto it. The other boys couldn't help but laugh in spite of Bobby's beet red face which usually signified that he was angry. Bobby curbed his temper however and smiled.

124

"That's right. Laugh it up ya fuckers," he said. "Just for that you guys can get the ATVs out of the truck you're own damned selves."

"But Bobby, you're so big and strong," taunted Denny in his best girlie voice while batting his eyelashes. Everyone laughed and then they unloaded the little quads. Bobby helped in spite of what he had just said. They loaded all of their gear onto the ATVs and then after a little arguing over who was going to drive, an argument which Denny and Shawn won, they were on their way.

26.

As they scooted along on the little ATVs the boys recognized a few areas marked by trees, gullies, and oddly shaped boulders from their hike with the scouts. They remembered how slow going the trip had been back then, and even considering the fact that they were using quads to quicken things up this time, they all knew now that they hadn't walked nearly as far as they had once thought, but back then everything had seemed bigger to them. When they hit the creek that spilled itself into the canyon far below, it too seemed a lot smaller. During the hike they had seen it more as a river than the little creek that it was, yet it was still just a little too big to cross with the ATVs.

"We can just go up stream until we find a place to cross," said Shawn.

They did just that and found a spot with a sort of sand bar before too long. By late afternoon they had reached the spot where they had camped out for the second night on the scout hike. They also found that someone else was there waiting for them.

In the exact place from where Shawn and Denny had followed Lester and Johnny that night, a small tent was set up, and sitting by a fire was a broad shouldered youth with platinum blonde hair. When the boys got to the fire they stopped the ATVs and the figure by the fire stood up.

"How are you guys doing?" He asked.

Denny knew that the young man who had just spoken was either Lester or Johnny Sabina, but he wasn't sure which. The last time he had seen them he had been able to tell them apart, but he could see that whichever this one was had changed since then. He had grown quite tall and had filled in admirably. He had also spoken, that was something that the twins had never done very much of, at least not other than to utter "quarter," when someone wanted to watch them eat something gross.

As if reading Denny's mind, the youth spoke again. "You're Denny Jackson," he said. "You've grown some, but I still recognize you. I imagine you all know that I'm one of the Sabina twins. I'm Johnny."

All four of the boys were thrown off by hearing Johnny speak, but after a moment Shawn finally managed to say the first thing that came into his mind, "where's Lester?"

Johnny turned towards the tent, and as if on command, his mirror image emerged. Lester quickly scanned the faces of their visitors and then joined them. "You're here for the same reason we are," he stated.

"What reason would that be?" Asked Bobby.

Lester smiled and reached into his pocket where he fished something out that he held up for everyone to see, -- a small, gold nugget.

Denny and Shawn quickly looked at each other with a mildly puzzled expression. Johnny caught their look and smiled. "Yes, it's the same one that you thought you saw me eat."

"You didn't really eat it?" Asked Denny.

"No, I just slipped it under my tongue."

"But you stuck your tongue out and wagged it right at us."

"Yes, but it was under there the same as a lot of the bugs and things that you thought you saw us eat," said Johnny.

"We only really ate a few of those bugs," said Lester, "and most of those were by accident."

"But it looked so real," said Bobby. "We all thought that you two were nuts."

"We liked to let people think that," said Johnny.

"Where did you get that gold?" Asked Shawn, "did you guys find the mine?"

"We found it on a ledge on the canyon wall," answered Lester. "We didn't find the mine, but we're pretty sure that it's down there somewhere, and probably not too far from that ledge."

"How did you know why we came here?" Asked Denny.

Johnny shrugged, "why else would you come here?"

No one said anything else for a moment. Denny and his group were trying to decide what to make of the unexpected discovery of the twins and of how they now seemed much more normal than they once had.

"You guys can camp here if you want," said Johnny. "As long as we're all here for the same thing we might just as well join forces."

Denny looked over at Shawn who had Carl on the back of his ATV. "What do you think?" He asked.

Shawn shrugged and then Bobby got off of the quad that Denny had been driving.

"We might as well," said Bobby. "If we're all here for the same thing we're going to run into each other sooner or later anyway."

That was good enough for Denny, Shawn, and Carl.

The clearing the twins had set their camp up in was a good site and they were all curious to get to know the new, improved, and *speaking* Johnny and Lester Sabina. They quickly set up their tents and then gathered more wood for the fire. They were expecting to be up until late

128

into the night talking about their chances of finding gold. Denny was considering whether or not to let the others in on Shawn and his encounter with Jake's ghost.

That might get the twins talking about the shit hawk, he thought.

He couldn't help but think that the giant sea gull that had seemed to have been leading the Sabina brothers that night knew where the mine was. He knew that believing a bird could possibly know such a thing was a ridiculous idea, but then again, a lot of the things he had already seen would have seemed ridiculous if he hadn't experienced them first hand.

When the boys had finished settling into camp, and after they had finished eating, they all sat around the fire.

Carl dug through his back pack and pulled out a package that contained a few cigars. Denny and the others watched as he stuck one into his mouth and lit it using a piece of wood that he had pulled out of the fire. The others could see that Carl was trying to kid himself into thinking that he was looking nonchalant and sophisticated, but to them, or to anyone else had they been able to see, the cigar only made what already was a baby face look even younger. It was obvious that if Carl had ever smoked in his life before tonight it hadn't been very often.

"What the fuck is that?" Asked Bobby.

"What's what?" Said Carl, still trying to pretend that for him to be smoking a cigar was the most natural thing in the world.

"You know what," said Bobby. "That fucking thing hanging out of your ugly mug, that's what."

"What's it look like?"

"It looks like a muddy dick to me," said Bobby.

129

All of the boys including Lester, Johnny, and Carl himself couldn't help but laugh at that last remark.

"How long have you been smoking those things?" Asked Bobby.

"I don't know," answered Carl, "a while now I guess."

"It makes you look like an ass hole," Bobby went on, "and the cigar looks like a turd."

All of the boys were laughing pretty hard now, and as Carl gasped for a breath he inhaled a lot of smoke and went into a coughing fit. This caused the rest of them to laugh harder still. When he finally gained control of his lungs again, Carl was feeling a little woozy. "I guess these things are kind of gross aren't they?"

"Yep, and they smell like shit," said Shawn.

"Want one?" Asked Carl.

"No thanks," answered Shawn.

"I'll have one," Denny cut in.

"Give me one too," said Bobby.

"I thought you said people smoking cigars looked like ass holes," said Carl.

"No, I said that *you* looked like an ass hole."

They all laughed again and Carl tossed a cigar to both Denny and Bobby.

"I brought something too," said Bobby after he lit his cigar. Then he went to the tent where his back pack was and returned with a forty ounce bottle of Jack Daniel's.

"Where'd you get that?" Asked Carl.

"Dad's liquor cabinet."

Denny knew Bobby's dad fairly well, he was the manager at Spencer's. "Won't he find out?" He asked.

"Nah," said Bobby, "he's got a few more bottles at home. My uncle keeps giving him Jack Daniel's for

Christmas and stuff, but dad only drinks beer. He won't notice if one is missing." Then Bobby twisted off the cap and took a swig of the whiskey right out of the bottle. "Want some?" He asked to no one in particular holding out the bottle.

"No mix?" Asked Shawn.

"You're supposed to drink JD straight," said Carl who had just appointed himself an expert on the subject. Then he took the bottle from Bobby and took a large swig, wincing at the taste.

The boys passed the bottle around, all of them taking drinks and then they got to talking about a variety of subjects including a debate over which girl in school they figured had the nicest ass. Finally they got to talking about what had brought them all out here in the first place.

"So where is this ledge you found the gold on?" Asked Carl of the twins.

"Not too far from here," said Lester, "we can show you tomorrow if you want."

Carl nodded, then Denny thought that this might be a good time to try to get the twins to talk about some of the other questions he had on his mind. "What made you go down there in the first place?" He asked.

Lester and Johnny looked at each other, then Johnny shrugged, "you already know, don't you?"

"Maybe, but let's hear it."

"You and Shawn both saw the shit hawk didn't you?"

It was the Jackson brothers turn to take a glance at each other, then they both nodded.

"Shit hawk?" Asked Bobby, "what shit hawk?"

Denny was just about to explain to Bobby all about the giant sea gull when Johnny spoke up for him. "Do you remember the story that old lady in the museum told us about Jake Vollmer claiming to have had his eye removed by a giant sea gull?"

"Yeah," said Bobby, "but Jake was nuts."

"Maybe," said Johnny, "but there really is a big sea gull flying around out here."

"Aw, c'mon," said Bobby. "You guys know that all of that is just a legend."

"We saw it too," said Shawn.

Denny nodded in confirmation.

"Naw," said Bobby, but the two Jacksons and the Sabina twins all nodded in unison. Bobby knew that Shawn and Denny didn't know the twins well enough to collaborate on such a tale unless there was some truth to it. "What's the shit hawk got to do with the gold mine?"

"We don't know," said Johnny, "but the night we camped here when we were with scouts, that shit hawk kept flying around here."

"I never heard it," said Bobby.

"Me either," said Carl, eager to agree with his idol.

"I think only me, Shawn, and the twins did," said Denny. "I heard it the night before that too."

"So when it flew away you just decided to follow it?" Asked Bobby.

"Sometimes me and Johnny feel things," said Lester, "and sometimes we know things that we shouldn't. We knew that the seagull wanted us to follow it."

"Why would a shit hawk want you to follow it?" Asked Carl in a sarcastic tone.

"That we don't know," said Johnny, "but we followed it anyway. It would fly off a little distance, then come back over us, and then fly off in the distance again. We followed it a ways right down into the canyon, but once

132

we got as far as that ledge we couldn't follow it any further without using a rope or something."

"And that's when you found the gold?" Asked Bobby.

"Yes," answered Lester.

There was a pause in the conversation that lasted for a long moment before Denny said, "you said that sometimes you guys know things that you shouldn't. What did you mean by that?"

"I guess it's kind of like intuition," said Johnny.

"Yeah, only different," said Lester.

"Can you two really read each other's minds?" Asked Denny.

Slowly the twins nodded.

"What about other people? Can you read other people's minds too?"

"Sometimes," said Johnny. "Not that often anymore."

"What do you mean not often anymore?" Asked Denny.

"Some people are easier to read than others," answered Johnny. "Some we can't read at all, and some people we can only read when they're either in deep thought or under duress. People who are angry or scared are the easiest, especially if they're easy to read to begin with."

The boys sat quietly for a while trying to digest what Johnny had just told them, then Lester continued on where his brother had left off.

"For a while there, when we were just beginning puberty, we could read almost everyone around us quite strongly, as a matter of fact, it was driving us nuts. We had a hard time concentrating on anything because we had so

133

many thoughts from other people's minds going through our heads."

"Wow," said Carl, "is that why you went away?"

Lester and Johnny thought about this for a moment before Johnny answered. "I would have to say yes. Our parents knew that we could read each other's minds, we've always been able to and when we were really young we never thought to try to hide that fact, but they didn't know that we could read their minds and others as well. When we started reading thoughts without even trying or wanting to, we were too distracted all the time and we know that our behavior was getting pretty strange. Mom and Dad sent us to a shrink to try to find out what was going on and we told him everything. We were very lucky that they had chosen the shrink that they did because another shrink might have tried to cash in on us and our abilities. It would have been easy for them to have furthered their careers by publishing papers and such on us. We probably would have become celebrities in the process, but we would have been miserable. Dr. Brighton, the psychiatrist our parents picked, did immediately become fascinated by us when he discovered that what we had told him was true, and he wanted us to go to a special school in Tamarack where we could keep a low profile, and where we would be close enough for him to study us in detail."

"So that's where you guys disappeared to," said Carl.

"Yes," said Lester, "and we're trusting you guys not to mention any of this to anyone. Dr. Brighton told us to keep our ability to ourselves. He said that if it got around that we really could read minds there would be a lot of people who would want us to do things for them and our lives would never again be our own."

134

"What people?" Asked Bobby, "want you to do what?"

"The government mostly," said Johnny. "Dr. Brighton said that quite a few departments of the government would love to get their hands on anyone who could read minds. Think about the FBI for example, they could interrogate crime suspects while we were present and we'd be able to tell them everything the suspect knew. We'd probably be able to help them find anyone the government was looking for."

"Like Bin Ladin or Hussein," blurted Carl.

"Yep," said Lester.

"But maybe you should help them find people like that," said Shawn. "You could do a lot of good."

"Dr. Brighton said he had thought about that for a long time too, but he said that as his patients, he should be looking out for our best interests. He also said that he thought that we were pretty young to get involved with all of that stuff, and that he had to respect the doctor/patient ethics of confidentiality."

"That would be pretty freaky shit!" Said Carl.

"Yeah, but now that we can't read minds nearly as good as we once could, we might not be able to help them all that much anyway," said Johnny. "Dr. Brighton did a lot of research while we were there on mind reading, premonition, and a lot of other things like that and he said it is very common for this type of phenomenon to be at it's strongest with young people during puberty. He said that a lot of these people lose their special abilities completely afterwards."

"But you two can still read minds sometimes?" Asked Denny.

The twins nodded. "Yes, and we've read some more things about ESP on our own, we wanted to learn as much about it as we could," said Lester. "We think that how strong the signals we receive are have a lot to do with an individuals electromagnetic fields and shit like that. Some people have much stronger fields than others. We're pretty sure that these same people are more likely than most to attract ghosts and have the ability to see them as well."

Lester looked directly at Denny as he said this and it made Denny feel very uncomfortable. He had the feeling that Lester was inside his head.

"Ghosts!" Snorted Bobby, "there's no such thing. You two really had me going there for a while, but you're just telling one of those campfire stories like Denny likes to tell. If you can really read minds then why don't you tell me what number I'm thinking about right now?"

"You're one of the one's that we could hardly ever read even at our strongest," said Johnny.

"Just like I thought," said Bobby. "You can't do it. You're just shooting us all a line of shit."

"Why do you think it is that Denny is so good at making up stories?" Asked Lester.

"Because he's got a good imagination," answered Bobby.

"Partly," said Johnny. It was strange talking to the twins. It was like talking to one mind shared by two bodies. One would pick up on the conversation exactly where the other had left off, "but some of those stories more than likely are from bits and pieces of things that he's picking up from the other side. A lot of artistic people are like that."

"I think you mean *autistic*," said Bobby, "not *artistic,* then he paused. "What other side?"

136

"The other side from life."

"Death?"

"No, not death. Nothing really dies, not like you think anyway," said Lester.

"There's no such thing as death?" Said Bobby.

"No, you just pass through."

"Through what?"

"Just through to the other side."

"What's on the other side?"

"No one knows until they get there."

Bobby laughed, "you're not making any sense."

"It's hard to explain," said Johnny, "and we only know a little bit of it."

"How do you guys know about this stuff?" Asked Shawn.

"We picked it up through other people," said Johnny, "people with that electromagnetic thing going on."

"Like who?" Asked Carl.

"Like Denny, he's *really* wired."

Denny had been quiet while he listened to the strange conversation. He wasn't enjoying this topic at all. "You can still read my mind?" He asked.

The Sabina brothers nodded.

Denny almost asked them to tell him what he was thinking about now, but then he thought better of it, he still had that feeling that someone was in his mind and it was scaring him. He didn't want to know that they could read minds. Instead he asked, "can you read thoughts from the other side?"

"Not really," said Lester. "We sort of can indirectly sometimes through other people. Like when you and Shawn saw Jake's ghost."

137

Denny's face paled. To him this was further proof of Lester and Johnny's abilities, it cast aside any room for doubt. Shawn wore an awkward expression as well. "How do you know about that?" He asked.

"It was impossible for us not to know," said Johnny. "That was when we were at our strongest at reading thoughts. Denny was always the easiest person to read that we've known, and he was scared at the time, that makes the signal stronger still. It was like he was standing beside us and screaming his thoughts into our ears."

For a moment Denny wanted to hop onto his ATV and head for home.

"So what was Jake thinking?" Asked Carl.

"He was confused," said Johnny. "He's done on this side, but he hasn't passed through yet and he doesn't know that he's supposed to."

"Was he thinking about where his mine was?"

"We don't know, it doesn't work that way with spirits, we could only get Denny's interpretation of Jake's thoughts," said Johnny.

"Is that what you thought Denny?" Asked Carl.

"Yes," answered Denny.

"Me too," said Shawn.

"There's another," said Lester suddenly in an excited tone.

"Another what?" Asked Bobby.

"Mind reader," answered Johnny. The way one of the twins picked up the conversation where the other had left off really was strange. To make it stranger still, they never disagreed with or interrupted one another. It really was like talking to one mind shared by two bodies.

"Where?"

"We don't know, somewhere not too far from here, he's trying to read Denny. I think we might have attracted him there."

"Do you know who it is?"

"No," answered Johnny. "It's only the second time we've ever felt another. This one is stronger than us, dark - - wait." A sudden look of concern crossed his face.

The twins became silent, faced each other, and closed their eyes. It appeared to the other boys that they were in some sort of a trance. Beads of sweat began to appear on their foreheads and upper lips, glistening in the fire light. The perspiration increased quickly and spread until their entire faces were shimmering.

"What are they doing?" Asked Carl.

"Shhh," hissed Bobby loudly, and Carl shut up.

All that could be heard now was the crackling fire and the crickets in the darkness skirting their camp. Whatever it was that Johnny and Lester were doing, it seemed to be requiring a lot of exertion. They both now had their hands on their faces with their index fingers pressed against their temples. The other boys watched in confused fascination.

After perhaps a little more than five minutes, the twins snapped out of their trance.

"What was that all about?" Asked Bobby.

"Whoever, or maybe we should say *what*ever it was that we detected doesn't want anyone around here," said Lester.

"He doesn't seem to know for certain that we're here," continued Johnny. "It seemed that he was just scanning."

"What did you mean by saying *what*ever it was?" Asked Bobby.

139

"It was something different from us," said Lester. "Something different from all of us."

"What the fuck is that supposed to mean?" Asked Bobby. He was getting annoyed by all of this talk about super natural mumbo jumbo. He could accept that they truly seemed to be able to read minds, or at least each other's and Denny's anyway, but now they were taking their little act too far. *They're trying to play us for fools,* he thought.

"He's not from this side," continued Lester.

"Oh, I see, now you've decided that you can read ghosts minds after all," said Bobby while rolling his eyes.

"No, we can't read his mind, we can only detect his presence, and he's really not from the other side either. He's from somewhere in the middle. He's never really been alive. Not like we are anyway."

"*What*? What the fuck is the middle?"

Johnny and Lester paused knowing that Bobby wasn't believing any of this and they could see that he was beginning to get pissed off. Finally in a quiet voice Johnny said, "evil."

Bobby grunted and took a last swig from the bottle of Jack Daniel's. "That's enough ghost stories for me tonight," he said. "I'm going to bed." Then he got up and disappeared into his tent.

The rest of the boys didn't know what to say. None of them were accustomed to alcohol and they had quickly gotten a good buzz from the JD. Sleep wouldn't be hard for them to find tonight.

"So," said Carl. "Evil's in the middle?"

"That's the best way we can put it," explained Johnny. "Entities that have never really walked the earth, and aren't of the other side. They're almost always malicious."

Carl was normally pretty gullible, but even he was having a hard time accepting this. He nodded, not wanted to create an argument, the expression on his pudgy face betrayed his desperate desire to either understand what they were trying to tell him or to say something to the contrary. The expression he wore would have caused Shawn and Denny to laugh had they not been so immersed in their own confusion.

"I think I'm going to turn in too." Said Carl, then it was just the Jacksons and the Sabinas left by the fire.

They sat in silence for a while before Denny asked, "was someone else really trying to read my mind?"

Lester nodded, "I think that if someone is already reading your mind it makes the path easier for others who can to get in there. I think we also threw him off."

"You two were reading my mind?"

Both Lester and Johnny looked a little embarrassed, like they had just gotten caught masturbating or something.

"Well quit it," said Denny. Then after a moment he added, "what do you mean it threw him off?"

"The same thought energy being picked up by three minds," said Johnny. "It sort of blocked him, or filtered your mind enough to keep him from really being able to get in. He probably thinks we're farther away from him than we really are so he's not worried about us enough to keep trying."

"All of this is just a little too much weird shit for us to easily swallow," said Shawn.

"We know," said Lester.

"You said that it was the second time you had come across another mind reader," said Denny. "When was the first?"

"At the museum," said Lester.

"That creepy old lady?" Asked Denny.

"Yes," said Johnny. "She seemed quite interested in you."

"She really gave me the willies," said Denny. "What was she thinking?"

"We don't know," answered Lester. "We couldn't read her at all."

"I wonder if she knows about all of this weird shit that goes on out here," said Shawn.

"I wouldn't bet against it," said Johnny.

"It's funny," said Denny. "I've never seen her before or after that day in the museum."

Neither Shawn or the twins had either.

27.

Dawn had come quite some time ago, and Mala, who was normally asleep by now, was still fretfully awake. During the night that had just passed she had again taken to wandering. She had been unable to help herself. In spite of her mother's stern warnings and the harsh consequences that were waiting should she ever be caught for going outside of the canyon, she just could not resist the urge to taste the freedom she felt on these short forays into the outside world, a world that she was sure was so much larger than that of which she knew.

Mala's mother had been waiting her return again this time, but this time she had no warning for her daughter. Instead there were tears in her eyes, Mala would have preferred a scolding.

"I'm sorry mother," she said. "I didn't go far. No one knows that I was gone."

Mala was telling the truth, she hadn't gone far. She had thought about trying to follow the canyon along the upper edge just to see how long it was, but after she had gone only a short way and with no end in sight, she knew that it would take far too long to find the end of it, and had returned home before she was missed.

Her mother waved her off. "That is only of secondary concern now," she told her.

"Why? What's wrong?"

"You are to be married."

"What? To Whom? When?"

"Within the next few days. Preparations are being made now."

143

Mala's mother stopped there seemingly not wanting to say anything further. It was not unusual for women of the Sasquatch tribe to be the last to know of their own upcoming nuptials, but there were always suitors beforehand and the woman in question had to at least make some sort of indication that she was interested in the prospective husband. Oddly in Mala's case, as beautiful as she was, she'd had no such suitors. Mala had never been able to understand why this was. Although she did keep herself hidden much of the time, she did mingle with others of her tribe when The Other was away. There were a few young males that she was interested in and she could tell by the way they looked at her that they were interested in her too, but so far none had courted her.

Mala's heart began pounding. Her mother's reaction to what had just been revealed let Mala know who it was that she was to be married to and she was terrified. Still she had to hear it, "to who mother?" She repeated.

"The Other," whispered her mother and she began to sob.

Mala's legs turned to rubber and she sagged to the floor where she sat with her knees drawn and her face cradled in her arms.

No ... no ... no, she thought, but somewhere deep inside her she had always known that this had been what was to come.

NOOOO! The thought screamed through her mind. *This isn't right, it's not fair.*

Now as Mala lay quietly pitying herself for the dismal fate that awaited her, she thought about the great pains she had taken to avoid being seen by The Other. All of the weddings and other merry gatherings that she had kept herself from. All of that time she had felt like an outsider amongst her own people merely because she had been brought into this world possessing such great beauty. A beauty that would have been envied anywhere else in the world, but here in the canyon, under fear and the watchful eye of something that wasn't even human, a curse. An entire childhood wasted in hiding had been all in vain. The constant worry and care that she had taken now only proving to have been wasted years of happiness, or at least as close to happiness as what came to her people. All because of one moment of carelessness when she allowed herself to be seen. Her remaining years she knew, would be filled with misery and the best that she could hope for was to go insane quickly to save herself from the reality of being a wife of The Other.

What Mala didn't know was that The Other had always known about her. He had known about her even before he had seen her on the ledge that night. When her body had made it's changes that brought her into womanhood, he had lusted after her. He had even stood by the very spot where she now lay and watched her as she slept. He had craved to touch her. *Not now,* he had told himself, *soon enough.*

Soon enough had almost arrived.

28.

"What a fucking mess in there," Bobby told the twins as he emerged from the tent that he had been sharing with Carl. "You two don't sleep much do you?"

Lester and Johnny had been up long enough to stoke the fire and shake that dopey, "I just got up," appearance. Then again, no one ever saw the twins with that dopey, I just got up appearance. Their hair and clothes looked immaculate as always.

"Carl threw up," said Lester.

"Yeah, it reeks too," said Bobby. Then after a pause he added, "hey, how did you know?"

The twins only looked at each other.

"You've got that mind reading thing going on again don't you?"

"Sorry," said Johnny. "Ever since we got near the canyon it's been stronger than it has been in a long time."

"Yeah, yeah," said Bobby. He was thinking that Lester and Johnny had probably just heard Carl heaving in the night and were only trying to feed him some more of their hocus pocus mumbo jumbo. He was about to ask them what he was thinking now.

"Seven," said Johnny.

Bobby had almost made it to the fire. He stopped in his tracks. Hearing Johnny say what he'd been thinking was really unnerving. The last shred of doubt he'd had about the twins abilities had just been erased.

"OK," he said, "I believe you. Now cut it out." He thought for a moment and then added, "I thought you said that you couldn't read my mind."

"We never could before now," said Lester.

146

Bobby filled up a tin coffee pot with water from a big jug that they had brought along on one of the ATVs and set it on the fire. Soon afterwards Denny and Shawn were awake. When Denny had himself settled with a cup of coffee in his hand the twins told him they had some news for him.

"What kind of news?" Denny asked.

"About the naked girl," said Lester.

Denny's mind was still clouded with sleep and it took a while for him to figure out what they were talking about. Finally it occurred to him who it was that they meant.

"From that night on the hike?"

The twins nodded.

"We'd all but forgotten about her," said Johnny.

"What girl?" Asked Bobby.

Denny and Shawn related their tale to Bobby about the beautiful young girl that they had seen on the night the twins had found the gold nugget. Bobby listened intently. There was so much of this mystic crap being thrown his way that it was very hard for him to swallow all of it, but after the twins had proven to him once and for all that they really could read minds he decided that it was better not to doubt anything anymore. He was going to have to trust his old and his newfound friends that everything they were telling him was true, no matter how unbelievable it all was.

"Do you remember when we told you that you have always been the easiest for us to read?" Lester asked Denny.

Denny nodded.

"There was one other that was just as easy."

"That girl, right?" Said Denny.

147

"Yes," said Johnny. "Only it's harder for us to decipher what she's thinking. A lot of people's thoughts come to them in words. Mala doesn't speak English."

"Her name is Mala?"

The twins nodded.

"People also think in pictures though," said Lester, "and we can pick up on emotional stress like fear or anger. Mala is very afraid right now."

"She's still around here?" Asked Denny.

"She lives near here," said Johnny, "in a cave along the canyon wall."

"Why's she livin' all alone in a cave?" Asked Bobby.

"She's not alone," answered Lester.

"Who's with her?"

"A whole bunch of people," answered Johnny. "Do you remember hearing about the Sasquatch Indians and how it is believed that it is still possible for them to still be around somewhere in Sasquatch National Park?"

"Yes," said Bobby.

"Well, now we all know where they are."

"Mala's a Sasquatch Indian?" Asked Denny.

"Me and Johnny think so," said Lester.

"I thought they were cannibals," said Denny.

"They are."

"She doesn't look like a cannibal to me."

"What does a cannibal look like?" Asked Johnny.

"I don't know, but I don't think they look like her."

"She is a hottie isn't she," said Lester. "It's funny how much she looks like Nicole isn't it?"

Denny blushed. He had been trying not to think about Nicole, it was too depressing, and he had always

148

known that Nicole looked an awful lot like the girl he had seen hiding in the tall grass that night on the scout hike.

"We know that you've got a thing for Mala," continued Johnny, "even if you won't admit it we know. We knew you had a crush on her that very first night. As far as we can tell, Mala herself has never eaten anyone, but her people do."

"Who do they eat?" Asked Bobby.

"You guys all know that a lot of people go missing in the park every year right?"

"Yes," answered Bobby, "but that's bound to happen in a park this size. The forest is so thick, people just get lost."

"Probably some do," said Johnny, "but we know that the Sasquatch Indians take people if they get too close to their camp."

Carl finally emerged from his tent, he didn't look like he was feeling much better than he must have felt when he had thrown up in the night.

"Hey ya fucker!" Hollered Bobby. "You've got a mess to clean up in there."

"Ya, I know," said Carl. "I need coffee first."

The other boys couldn't help but stare at Carl. Carl couldn't be described as good looking during any time of the day, but he really looked like shit in the morning, and his hang over was making him look even worse.

"When are we going to look for the mine?" Carl asked.

"As soon as you're ready sunshine," answered Bobby.

The Sabina twins and the Jackson brothers all laughed at this, then they got him up to speed on what they had all been talking about.

149

"Maybe we shouldn't go down there," said Carl. "Maybe we should go back to town and tell the cops what we know."

"Yeah right," said Bobby, "like they're going to believe us."

After Carl had a moment to think about this, he realized that Bobby was right. He could just imagine Constable McClean's reaction to them telling him that they knew that there were cannibals in Reid's Canyon because Lester and Johnny could read minds and they said so.

"Even still," said Carl, "wouldn't it be kind of stupid for us to go down there knowing that we could get eaten?"

"Do you think after all these years of being so stupid you should try to start making sense now?" Said Bobby laughing.

"The Sasquatch Indians only come out at night," said Lester. "They sleep, hidden away during the day."

"But what if they hear us?" Asked Carl

"They won't if we put a muzzle on your ugly mug," said Bobby, "and think of how rich we'll all be if we find that gold mine."

"Hey," Denny interrupted, he looked at the twins, "you didn't say what it was that Mala was afraid of."

Lester and Johnny looked at each other as if they were deciding on which of them was going to reply and then Johnny spoke.

"She's getting married."

Denny felt a pang of jealousy as he again pictured her beautiful face. He thought that she was a little young to be getting married, but he knew that in the olden days, all Indian women were married young.

"Why would she be afraid of that?" He asked.

150

"Because she has to marry that other mind reader that we told you about," answered Lester.

"But I thought you said that he's not even human," said Carl.

"He's not."

"That's kind of fucked up then isn't it?" Said Carl. It was a question that didn't need an answer.

"How do you know about all of this?" Asked Denny.

"We picked up her thoughts this morning," answered Johnny. "She's scared, so it was easy. A lot of what she was thinking was in words, but there were enough pictures in there for us to be able to understand what was going on."

"Do you know what she is thinking now?"

29

A plan suddenly came to Mala as she lay awake thinking about her dismal future. *What is stopping me from running away? The worst thing that could happen to her was that she would be caught and either forced to marry The Other or be eaten.*

As far as she was concerned, death was a lot more desirable than spending the rest of her days as a wife of The Other.

Where would I go? I guess it really doesn't matter as long as it's away from here.

Mala was more than capable of surviving in the wilderness alone. All of her people learned how to live off the land as soon as they were capable of being taught. All she had to do was to get far enough away from the canyon that the hunters wouldn't follow her. They were slaves to their territory which really wasn't very broad. She could find out where the outsiders lived and set up a camp of her own near them. Her people were so scared of being discovered by the outsiders that they wouldn't dare to venture too close to wherever it was that they lived. She would be safe. Mala knew how to make her trail difficult to follow. The hunters were experts at tracking, but she knew enough to follow streams and to travel on rocky areas whenever possible. All she had to do was make it out of the canyon. If she could do that, then from there on she was relatively confident that she could make good her escape.

Mala quickly packed her few belongings into a bundle secured with leather straps. Silently, she went to the other side of the small cave from her bed to where her mother was sleeping.

I'm going to miss you mother, Mala thought as a tear trickled down her cheek. She didn't think that there would be much else of the only life she'd ever known that she would miss however.

The brightness outside of the dark cave took a moment to adjust to, and Mala waited by the mouth until her eyes tolerated the light. She stepped out and turned to her right intending to go to her ledge from where she would scale the canyon wall for the last time, but then her eyes caught a figure sitting motionless. His back against the canyon wall, and his eyes glued to her, sat The Other, precisely the last thing in the world she wanted to see, especially at this particular time.

Mala gasped when she saw him, and The Other gave her a lecherous grin. In his eyes she saw that he knew exactly what she was up to. She had been caught red handed.

The Other clapped his hands together a single time, and from behind a clump of bushes next to where The Other was sitting came the chief and two other men.

Mala stood rooted in silence. Without any words being exchanged, the two men with the chief walked to either side of her where they each held an arm and took her away.

30

Carl cleaned the puke out of the tent. For a moment he was certain that he was going to hurl again as the acrid smell caused his stomach to churn, but the moment passed and by the time he was done he looked as close to alert as he ever did.

While Carl completed his task, the rest of the boys had put everything that they thought they might need into backpacks and then they were ready. Briefly they considered trying to cram all six of themselves onto the two little ATVs and drive closer to the spot where Lester and Johnny said the ledge where they had found the gold nugget was, but it was only a short distance away, easier for them to walk to.

Soon afterwards Denny found himself looking at the boulder where he and Shawn and Jake Vollmer had crouched behind as the shots rang out from trees not too far away. Although it was still quite an impressive size, it too looked smaller to him now than it had then. He scanned the area for any signs of Jake, but found none.

"The scene of the crime," said Johnny.

"Yes, I guess it is," said Denny.

"What are you guys talking about?" Asked Bobby.

Denny and Shawn told him all about their encounter with the ghost of Jake Vollmer.

"Remember that old lady in the museum?" Asked Carl.

They all did, that look she had given Denny at the end of her talk was something he didn't think he was ever going to forget.

"Well, she said that a lot of people tried to find Jake's mine after he came to town with that sack of gold."

"I'm sure we all remember what she told us," said Denny. "That old bat was creepy."

"Yeah, I thought so too," said Carl. "Anyway, I think I know why so many of those people never came back."

"'Cause Jake shot 'em," interrupted Shawn.

"Uh huh," said Carl. "I bet that's what you saw that night. Jake shooting squatters."

"I think they already figured that much out ya brainiac," said Bobby.

"I wonder how many squatters Jake shot before they finally got him," said Shawn.

They all looked at Lester and Johnny expecting them to have the answer.

"Don't look at us," said Lester. "We don't know.

The boys continued south for a short distance.

"Here it is," said Johnny.

All of the boys except for the Sabina twins had pictured a nice wide ledge, easy to walk on, that would take them from the top of the canyon to the bottom. What they saw instead was a sheer rock wall broken only by a series of small ledges. These ledges were perhaps four to six inches in width.

"See that wide one way down there?" Asked Lester.

The Jackson's, Bobby, and Carl all peered down cautiously. None of them were very good at judging depth and their estimates for the canyon's depth ranged from two hundred to five hundred feet. The actual depth of the canyon at this spot was much closer to the latter. More than half way down, the boys saw a ledge that was much wider than any of the others they could see, somewhere between four and five feet. This ledge was also maybe ten feet across and had shrubs growing on either side of it.

When the boys indicated that they could see the ledge, Lester continued. "That's where we found the gold."

"How the fuck did you get down there?" Asked Carl.

"How else? We climbed," answered Johnny.

"Holy shit," said Carl peering downwards again, "you guys are fucking nuts."

"What possessed you to go down that far?" Asked Bobby.

"The shit hawk," said Lester. "It kept flying around in circles over us and then it landed down there."

"And you two figured that it was a good idea to risk your necks and climb down the canyon wall just because a shit hawk landed on a ledge?"

Lester and Johnny looked at each other, "yep," they answered.

Bobby, Shawn, and Denny laughed.

"You guys are all fucking nuts, said Carl. "I'm not going down there."

"It's really not as hard as it looks as long as you don't look down," said Lester. "And there are all kinds of nooks and crannies to hold on to. All you have to do is go at a nice, slow, and steady pace."

Hearing this Bobby stripped off his back pack. "It would probably be better not to try and lug these things down there," he said.

"It'd be a lot better not to lug our hairy asses down there at all," said Carl.

"Pussy," said Bobby, he was already lowering his feet over the canyon wall. He knew Carl well enough to know that he always put on a show when he didn't want to do something, but if someone called him a pussy or dared him to do something, Carl was unable to resist the challenge. Bobby had gotten Carl to do a lot of stupid things and Carl was so damned clumsy that it really was a wonder that he hadn't killed himself while procuring a number of these dares.

"If you fall, you'll die," said Carl.

"Then we better not fall," said Denny, who was also lowering himself over the edge of the canyon.

"Some of us might die," said Bobby, "but you'll just bounce with all of that flab you got on you."

"Ass hole!" Said Carl.

"If Lester and Johnny made it down there, then so can we."

"Ass hole," Carl whispered again, and then after everyone but him had disappeared over the edge he followed, muttering obscenities the whole time.

31.

Roughly at the center of the Sasquatch Indians'
caves, and at the base of the canyon, there was a hollowed
space in the rock. It looked as if a giant had taken his hand
and dug out a pocket in the canyon wall much the same as a
child might do while playing in the sand on a beach. The
difference being that a pocket dug at the base of one of the
walls in a sand trench would soon cave in. Rock held fast.

This hollowed out spot had been the Sasquatch
Indians common area since they had moved from what is
now Vollmer's Hollow and into the canyon. Here was
where they met as a community. It was where wedding
celebrations, trials, funerals, and feasts took place. This
hollow in the canyon wall, almost like a giant cave, was
where tribe members spent most of their waking hours. It
was where they had their meals, socialized, and otherwise
lived their day to day, or more accurately, night to night
lives.

The Indians had gone to great lengths to hide this
common area. They planted trees and dense brush at the
mouth to conceal it, and to a casual observer it would not
attract interest. From time to time planes and helicopters
flew overhead, but from the air it was invisible. Reid's
Canyon attracted quite a number of tourists each summer,
but most of these were happy enough to gaze at the
majestic spectacle from the lookout point not far from
where the loop was located and parking was available.
Some of the more adventurous visitors hiked along the
edge of the canyon at the top, but only a few of these made
it far enough to be close to the Sasquatch territory, but for
someone peering down into the canyon, even from it's lip,

158

there was no visible evidence of the hidden tribe's existence, and since these Indians were nocturnal, sightings were very rare.

Summer also brought a number of canoeists and kayakers down Reid's River, but as the river passed the Sasquatch territory, it became a rapids, and was a couple hundred yards away from the common area, those kayakers that were foolhardy enough to test their skills here were far too busy concentrating on keeping upright in the white water to pay much attention to the area around them. To further assist in their continued concealment was The Other's ability to detect any outsiders who ventured near, he was also able to detect when circumstances permitted capture of these outsiders, and the capture of an outsider always meant one thing, a feast.

There were a number of caves within the hollowed spot in the canyon wall, including a large one that contained a wooden cage where captives were held. Periodically this cage was also used to hold a tribe member who had been found guilty of one crime or another. Most crimes committed by Sasquatch Indians were punished in the same manner as outsiders were dealt with, they were cooked alive over an open fire and eaten. The Other always instructed that the victim be roasted in such a way as to keep him alive for as long as possible for the Other derived great pleasure in the extreme pain of others.

Mala now found herself within this cage, the same cage she had seen that terrified outsider in a few years earlier. She couldn't help but wonder if the same fate awaited her as what had befallen him. She remembered his cries of agony and had smelled the sickly sweet aroma of his roasting flesh that had seemed to permeate the entire canyon shortly afterwards.

159

When the feast was over the dead man had remained a source of food for her people for a couple of days afterward. His bones had been boiled to make soup, and Mala had even seen an old woman with no teeth sucking the marrow out of one of these bones after all of the meat had been stripped from it by the boiling water. The sight had sickened her.

As she had walked through the common grounds that day watching all of this, a day when The Other had gone somewhere outside of the canyon making it safe for her, Mala had remembered something else that her father had told her about The Other.

"He doesn't eat," he had said. "He takes great pleasure in watching us devour another human, but he never eats."

Mala remembered that it wasn't only human flesh that Takka had meant when he had talked to her. The Other never ate anything, no food at all, ever.

Mala was of course terrified of becoming the main course for her people's next feast. She tried to imagine what it would feel like to be strapped to a spit while hungry flames licked at her body. She trembled at the thought.

There's no way I can endure that kind of pain, she thought. She also knew however, that the decision was out of her hands. If The Other deemed it fit for her to die, then endure it she must, there was absolutely nothing she could do about it.

Mala had lost count of the number of times she had broken down into heart wrenching tears since her capture. Her stomach was in knots and the acrid taste of bile was in her mouth. Her crying had been so intense that already she had emptied her stomach three times. She was in the midst

160

of yet another weeping spell when she was permitted a visit, her mother.

Erenya looked crushed as she gazed at her beautiful, young daughter. She couldn't fathom what must be going through the girl's mind.

"I begged for mercy on your behalf," said Erenya. "As it turns out, it wasn't necessary. The Other is so taken with you that he has decided to spare you in spite of your attempted escape. What were you thinking? Surly you knew that you would be caught. The Other knows your mind. He knows all of our minds."

Mala had taken little comfort in her mother's words. True, when faced with her immediate and horrible death, she was relieved to find that she had avoided the incredible pain that she had been certain awaited her only moments ago, but she also knew why The Other had spared her even before her mother continued.

"You are to be married tomorrow night," said Erenya.

Which is worse? Wondered Mala, *the excruciating pain of a slow death by fire would have been over in less than an hour, but what of a marriage to The Other? Years and years of insanity. What happened to those other poor women that was so terrible that it has broken their minds forever?*

With her throat raw from her intense sobbing, Mala found her voice, her words came out in a croak. "Maybe death would be better mother."

"No, don't say that," pleaded Erenya. "You must think positively."

"But you know as well as I do that I'm going to go mad. What kind of a life is that?"

161

"You must prepare yourself. Learn to put your mind outside of yourself. When The Other forces you to perform your wifely duties let your mind go somewhere else, maybe in this way you will be able to cope."

"Don't you see mother? All of The Other's wives have done just that, only their minds never came back."

"It can be different for you though Mala. If you can just prepare yourself you can survive in a way that the others have failed."

"I think mother," said Mala, "that after The Other has had you, you don't want to survive."

Now it was Erenya's turn to cry. "Please Mala, be strong. I'm sorry I couldn't protect you."

"It's not your fault, no one could have protected me. I love you mother."

With that, the chief's two henchmen entered the cave to escort Erenya out. Mother and daughter's eyes locked. Erenya's filled with desperation, and Mala's with resignation.

"Good bye mother," said Mala.

Erenya, still sobbing, said, "I love you too Mala. Be strong."

Mala was left alone to try and force herself to find hope in her mother's words.

32

"C'mon lard ass!" Yelled Bobby.

"I'm coming," said Carl. "I'm afraid of heights you know."

"All the more reason to hurry the fuck up and come down."

Bobby, the Jackson brothers, and the Sabina twins had all made it down to the wide ledge where Lester and Johnny had found the gold nugget and they were all staring up at Carl as he inched his way down the canyon wall towards them.

"Don't rag him too much," Denny whispered to Bobby. "You'll make the clumsy bastard fall."

After what had seemed an eternity, Carl finally made it down to the ledge with the others, he was huffing and puffing and sweating profusely.

"You look like you just saw God," said Bobby laughing.

Carl ignored him. He had a canteen strapped to a belt around his waist. He wriggled this free and gulped down more than half of it's contents.

"Easy there big fella," said Bobby. "Save some for later."

"There's a river down there," said Bobby. "I can fill it back up when we get there."

The others looked down at Reid's river. Already they could hear the water as it sped along at this section, white water boiling over rocks and other debris.

"Where was the nugget lying when you found it?" Asked Shawn.

"Over there by those bushes," said Lester nodding towards a clump of shrubs that clung to the canyon wall on the south side of the ledge.

Shawn moved to that side scanning the area as he went. He poked at the shrubs and said, "it doesn't look like there's any more, how do you suppose that nugget you found got up here?"

"Probably a bird or some -- ," Johnny began when they all heard a screech that was familiar to the Jackson's and the Sabina's. The boys turned towards the north where the sound had originated.

"What the fuck was that?" Asked Carl. "Was that the shit hawk?"

Denny nodded and a moment later the giant seagull came into view as it flew over the edge of the canyon and then directly towards them.

"The fucker's attacking," said Bobby, but the shit hawk swooped below them and continued south.

"That's the biggest shit hawk I've ever seen," said Carl. "I wasn't sure if you guys were shittin' us or not."

"Why would we shit you about something like that?" Asked Shawn, then he added, "I wonder why it flew down there."

"'Cause that's what shit hawks do," said Bobby.

"We should follow it," said Lester.

"Sounds like as good an idea as any," said Bobby, and the others all agreed.

"It looks like the going is easier from here," said Denny as he looked downward. The rest of the boys all saw what he meant. There were a lot of little ledges from here on, some sloping downwards for quite a distance. It was going to be like walking on a series of two by fours for the rest of the way down.

164

They had just resumed their descent with Lester and Johnny in the lead when the twins suddenly stopped dead in their tracks almost causing Denny to run right smack into Johnny.

"Hey! Watch what the fuck you're do ... ," Denny started, but he saw that Lester had quickly spun around to face his brother. The two now had their eyes tightly shut. They were doing their trance thing once again. The other boys remained quiet and watched.

They must have sensed that other mind reader again, thought Denny.

The twins stayed in this posture for two or three minutes. When they snapped out of it Shawn asked, "what was that all about?"

"The other mind reader," said Lester.

"Well ... ?" Said Bobby.

"He was scanning again, but we blocked him," said Johnny.

"What would happen if you didn't block him?" Asked Shawn.

Lester answered, "I don't think we want to find out."

"Maybe all of this is a bad idea," said Carl. "Maybe we should just go back."

Bobby looked upwards at the canyon wall. "That looks like an awful long way up from down here."

The others looked up as well. It hadn't seemed so far while they had been descending, but they all knew that when it was time for them to go back up it was going to be a different story. They all thought about what Carl had just said, they also thought about what the twins had been telling them about this other mind reader. More than one of the other boys was thinking that Carl's advise might not be

165

so ill-founded. Going in search of Jake's gold mine had sounded like something right out of a movie at first. Life in Vollmer's Hollow was so dull. A chance for them to go on a real live adventure had been irresistible, but now faced with what the twins seemed to think was a real danger, the boys weren't so sure. Everything the twins had told them so far, no matter how unbelievable, had been proven to be true. Did they really want to risk running into this other mind reader that Lester and Johnny seemed so afraid of?

As all of this was going on through the boys' minds their silence was broken by another screech in the distance. All six young men looked into the direction of the sound anticipating another glimpse of the giant shit hawk. Soon they saw it flying towards them.

"Here we go," said Bobby. "This time the fucker's going to attack."

But again Bobby was proven wrong. The seagull swooped in front of them and dropped something out of it's beak. The object bounced from a narrow ledge in front of them and landed on another only a few feet below. The object rolled and bounced a little more and then stopped just short of trickling off of this second ledge where it probably would have kept falling until it had reached the bottom of the canyon.

All of the boys knew what this object was even before Johnny made his way to it and held it up for their inspection. It was another gold nugget.

"I guess that explains how the other one you guys found got on the ledge," said Denny.

"The mine can't be too far away from here then," said Shawn. "It must be right down there somewhere." He pointed down into the direction of where the shit hawk had come from.

166

"It really does look like the going will be a lot easier the rest of the way down," said Carl.

"Yeah," said Bobby. "I guess it would be kind of stupid to come this far just to give up now wouldn't it?"

Gold has always had a strange effect on people, and Denny and company were no different than so many others before them in this respect. In their minds, a chance for untold riches far outweighed any possible hazards. The sight of another gold nugget that they were sure had come from somewhere within the canyon had the boys all but foaming at the mouth. No further words needed to be spoken, their decision had been made, they were going to continue with their search.

The longer the boys were on the canyon wall, and the closer they got to the bottom, the cockier Carl became in his rock climbing abilities, so cocky in fact that he had become quite reckless. Often times he walked too fast on the narrow series of ledges without bothering to use his hands on the wall for further support. He was taking far too many chances, and more than once he had stepped on Bobby's heels whom was in front of him. Carl had nearly caused Bobby to fall on one occasion.

"Settle down you clumsy bastard!" Bobby had warned.

"Sorry," said Carl. "I guess I'm just getting the hang of this faster than the rest of you."

Bobby had looked back at his flabby friend who was still sweating profusely and looked far from at home doing any kind of physical activity. "You're an ass Carl. Do you know that? You really are an ass. You're the clumsiest fucker I know, and now you think you're a fucking mountain goat."

Carl could see that Bobby was really getting pissed and thought it best not to say anything further.

When the boys had made it to within ten or twelve feet from the bottom, they heard a sudden scramble-scraping sound, and then a WHOMPF! It sounded like a large sack of sugar being dropped from a height.

"Stupid fucker!" Yelled Bobby. "I knew that was going to happen sooner or later."

The others who had been concentrating on the ledges and where each of their next footfalls were going to be looked around behind them to where Carl and Bobby where. They could see Bobby standing on a ledge looking down, but there was no sign of Carl, at least not until they followed Bobby's gaze. Rolling around on the ground in obvious pain on the canyon floor they saw him.

"Stupid bastard kept fucking around until he fell," said Bobby. "He's lucky it didn't happen when we were higher up."

They made their way to Carl's side as quickly as they could.

"You okay?" Asked Denny.

Carl's face was as white as a sheet and he was making a funny, dry, moaning sound.

"Got the wind knocked out of you didn't you?" Asked Bobby.

Carl nodded.

"Break anything?"

Carl shook his head.

"Too bad," said Bobby. "You damned near took me down with you."

After a few minutes Carl got his breath back.

"You okay now?" Asked Bobby.

168

Carl nodded. For once he was at a loss for words as he took a good razzing from his friends. Eventually the color came back into his face and then they continued south towards the protrusion on the canyon wall. As they rounded this they found a hollowed out area. It looked to Denny almost like a big dent in the rock. As they walked farther they found a clear space that was bordered on one side by the canyon wall and by trees, mostly evergreens on the other.

"Hey you guys," said Shawn. "I think that we're really close to it now," and without any of the others saying anything, he knew they all felt the same way.

33.

The Other was confused and he didn't like it. He was certain that he had found the mind of an outsider more than once over the last couple of days. He had been inside the minds of so many humans before that he knew he hadn't been mistaken, but before he had been able to detect the location of the signal it had become all jumbled. The Other sometimes picked up signals from animals, especially if they were in some sort of distress, and the fleeting human pattern he had sensed recently had changed into something more like that.

But that isn't possible, he thought. *Something is wrong here.*

This was greatly disturbing to The Other. He was never wrong. Ever.

Momentarily he thought about summoning the chief and having him send out hunters to see what they could find, but he didn't know where to send them.

It wouldn't do to have them go out and find nothing.

Previously, every time when he had sensed the presence of a near by outsider he had been correct and he had known the location as well. When the hunters had been sent, they had always returned with a captive. Always. One hundred percent.

No, it wouldn't do to send them out and have them come back empty handed. I can't have them thinking I was wrong about anything, ... ever! It takes very little to plant seeds of doubt into the minds of these stupid humans. If I'm proven wrong just once, it will nullify all of the times before when I've been right.

Any shadow of doubt cast upon The Other's abilities was to cast doubt upon The Other himself, and that wouldn't do. The Other had been around since the beginning of mankind, and he existed only because man wanted him to. Sure, man wanted to kid themselves into thinking that they were a species with hearts and souls that contained mainly good qualities like kindness and nobility, but The Other knew better. He knew what humans were really all about. Humans were a brutal, selfish lot. No matter what they said, they were concerned only about themselves. They were greedy too, not only were they in constant pursuit of worthless, worldly possessions, but they craved recognition from their fellow man. They persistently attempted to gain esteem and praise among others of their kind, seemingly ignorant to the fact that those very souls that they were trying to impress were only concerned about themselves and their own accomplishments. The Other found this to be hilarious.

They compliment one another when face to face only to try to grind each other's reputations into the ground when the opportunity to do so arises.

The Other loathed these foolish humans, but he also needed them, for he was borne of their darkest traits. He was an entity that had arose from nothing but their evil thoughts and deeds. An evil that each of these idiots didn't want to admit existed within themselves. He had to concede that the thoughts and imaginations of humankind were filled with endless possibilities.

If the fools would learn that if they were to channel the more positive thoughts to action, they could create for themselves lives filled with much more meaning than they believe possible.

171

Instead, they dwelt on the negative, the evil, and they wanted to believe so badly that this evil existed from somewhere outside of themselves that they had unwittingly created The Other, and more like him, from the sheer faith and negative energy generated from their minds.

As the years went by, The Other counted himself more and more lucky to have made himself a home with the Sasquatch Indians. He had been with them since the beginning of the tribe's existence. He remembered well how when many years ago, a group had strayed from their original tribe because of some ridiculous rift a few of them had had with their chief and elders. A few more than fifty of them had set off into the wilderness on their own in search of a suitable territory to claim as their own. They had misjudged the length of time it was going to take for them to find such a site however, and that winter they found themselves starving to death in the middle of a vast forest.

Humans, The Other had found, were quite resourceful when it came to matters of their survival, and these first members of the Sasquatch tribe had resorted to eating their dead in order that the better percentage of them could make it out of that first winter alive.

The Other had been able to read their anguished thoughts from far away. The horror and revulsion they had felt within themselves because of what they had done had practically screamed for him to come. They needed somewhere to place the severe guilt they felt, but couldn't deal with. They needed a savior of sorts, someone or something other than themselves to blame for what they had been reduced to.

The Other had gone to them that winter, but had remained hidden. He waited and watched until the souls of the Sasquatch were overflowing with darkness because of the revulsion they had directed towards themselves. When he finally presented himself to them that spring, they were more than ready to accept him, they were in desperate need of him.

Since that time, The Other had sensed a change in the world outside of the canyon where he and his chosen people had hidden themselves. Man had become increasingly evil, but at the same time had a more and more decreased sense of guilt about it. Except for extreme cases, humans no longer needed an outside entity to place the blame upon for their despicable actions. They had decided that they were now far too sophisticated to harbor any beliefs that such an entity could exist. They didn't believe in magic, and so many had lost faith in anything other than what they could see and touch for themselves that The Other had severe doubts that he could exist amongst them for long. He was certain that surrounded by such a disbelief in magic, good and evil, heaven and hell, or even the other side, would be cause enough for him to simply fade away.

All of this was the greatest reason for his desire to keep the Sasquatch Indians away from, and undiscovered by the outside world. They remained untouched by the rest of humankind's *"progress"*. These Indians were happy to believe in magic and to accept things that they didn't understand. To them the whole world was a mystical place, and in such an attitude, they kept The Other strong. Belief in magic and other unexplainable entities such as The Other, was to keep them alive, thus The Other was quite comfortable hidden away in the canyon with these people who believed.

173

The detection of an outsider had always been a cause for concern to The Other, but so far the method he had designed for dealing with them had proven to be quite effective. All he had to do was order the chief to summon the hunters and they had never failed to bring the trespasser in. This last detection however, was a cause for worry. What had happened? He was certain that he hadn't been mistaken, but why had he suddenly lost the signal? He hadn't picked up on the mind of someone in one of the outsider's flying machines had he? That could be a possible explanation, but no, that's not what had happened, he was sure of it.

The Other knew of only one way to deal with this problem without raising any questions from the Sasquatch. He was going to have to go out of the canyon and see if he could find the outsider himself. The Other of course, had been outside of the canyon many times before. Occasionally one of those extreme cases of guilt brought on by some unspeakable evil in the world outside would require his personal attention. Normally he enjoyed these outside excursions, they always left him hopeful that this loss in the belief of magic in the greater part of the world was only a temporary phase. This time it was different though, and with his next wedding so near, he was finding it to be quite irritating.

The Other had no need of food or sleep, but he was far from being above participation in pleasures of the flesh. He had always found the females of the human species to be irresistibly tantalizing. Mala was to be his greatest conquest yet, his most beautiful bride ever, and he couldn't wait to get the ceremony and the following celebration out of the way so he could begin his husbandly liberties with her.

First however, he had to make certain that the outsider he had detected was gone. His inability to remain inside of this outsider's mind frightened him, and if he found him, then he could summon the chief. This would cause a delay in his marriage to Mala, but The Other could see no other options. If he had been able to say in this outsider's mind he would have had no cause for alarm and may even have let him be, but a human who could jumble his brain waves so effectively was dangerous, and The Other would never feel comfortable again until this danger was erased.

34

When the boys entered the hollow in the canyon wall they all felt a strange sense that someone had been there not long before them. As they studied the ground it appeared to them to have that packed down look like an unpaved area got when it had seen heavy foot traffic over a long period of time. And what of those trees? From inside the hollow they provided a perfect barrier. Anyone traveling down the river would never be able to see the boys while they were in here. As a matter of fact, an onlooker would have been oblivious to the clearing behind the trees all together.

Denny couldn't help but think that he was standing on private ground. He was sure that this would be how it would feel if he were to enter someone's home while they were out, like a trespasser. He also knew that if he were to speak to any of the others while he was here it would be in a whisper.

While he was thinking this, Denny saw Shawn trying to gain his attention while he pointed at something on the ground. It appeared that Shawn didn't feel comfortable speaking too loudly here either, otherwise he would have hollered for every one to come and take a look at whatever it was that he had discovered.

As the boys neared Shawn they saw what it was that had attracted his attention, a large fire pit. Blackened remnants of still slightly smoking wood were surrounded by rocks. These rocks seemed to have been set into place with great care and formed a perfect circle.

Shawn whispered, "it looks like it's been here for a long time."

The others all quietly agreed. The rocks appeared to have worked their way into the ground, as if they had settled there after guarding the fire for centuries.

Denny, Shawn, and the rest of the boys scanned the area from where they stood for any other signs of humans. The ground was packed hard, but as they continued to look they found a few footprints that must have been left after a rain while the ground had still been wet and soft. It also seemed odd that these prints had been left by bare feet.

"Someone hangs out here quite a bit," whispered Carl. "Why would they come here?"

"Maybe they found the mine," said Bobby, also in a whisper.

"I'll bet that's where they are right now," said Carl. "We're too late, someone got here before us."

"Hey," interrupted Denny. "It looks like there's something behind that clump of bushes over there."

The others followed Denny's gaze and found a patch of shrubs growing by the canyon wall. Soon afterwards they understood what Denny had been talking about. There was a large crack in the rock wall behind the bushes. They walked over to it.

"Looks like a cave," whispered Carl excitedly.

"I wonder how far back it goes," said Bobby.

"It sure is dark in there," said Denny. "Did anyone bring a flashlight?"

Shawn and Bobby both had, Shawn pulled his out of a small pack and pointed it inside. What they saw looked more like a tunnel than a cave, and from the outside where the young men stood, there was no way of telling how long it was. This tunnel didn't look very inviting. It wasn't round like Denny had envisioned a tunnel ought to be, it was more like a ragged, narrow triangle.

As Shawn shifted the beam of the flashlight trying to get a better view inside they all saw something glitter on the tunnel's floor when the light passed over it.

"What was that?" Asked Bobby in a loud whisper.

Shawn moved the beam of light back to rest on it.

"That's gold," said Shawn. "This must be the mine!"

"Are you sure?" Asked Bobby.

"Sure I'm sure," answered Shawn. Then he handed his flashlight to Lester and went inside. His back brushed the roof of the tunnel as he made his way towards the glittering object and dirt fell. He stopped momentarily, a little nervous of a possible cave-in, but other than the dirt and dust, everything seemed to be holding OK. He quickly continued on his way, snatched up the glittery object, and came back outside.

"It is gold!" Said Bobby, forgetting to whisper this time. "Ha ha! We found it."

35.

It had been hours since Erenya had visited her daughter. It had been hours since Mala had seen anyone at all. Everyone was asleep, and Mala knew it would be quite a while longer before the sun went down and her people awoke. There would possibly be someone standing guard by the mouth of the cave that her and her cage was in, but even if there was, the sentry would be sleeping as well.

Mala felt more tired than she'd ever felt in her life, but was unable to sleep. She'd studied the cage closely. Although it was dim, enough light seeped into the cave for her to be able to see all of the joints of the wooden structure where she was being held captive. For all she hoped however, she was unable to find anything on the cage that she thought she might be able to pry lose with her bare hands and free herself. Finally she had given up.

Waiting for the time when she would be forced to the altar on a ledge above the community grounds was an ordeal Mala wouldn't have wished upon her worst enemy had she had one. Time dragged on, and yet each minute sped her closer to the dreaded moment when she would have to surrender her young body to The Other. This waiting was almost enough to drive her to the insanity that she knew awaited her after her marriage had been consummated.

While she sat on the rock floor of the cage pondering her bleak future, Mala was suddenly sure that she had caught the sound of a voice. It had been brief, but she was sure that she had heard a young man. The voice had been from outside, somewhere near by. It was hard to judge from which direction it had originated because sounds carried funny within the hollowed portion of the canyon wall. She sat rigidly for a while straining her ears to hear more, but whoever it had been was said nothing further.

Who could be out and about at this hour? She wondered.

Although it wasn't forbidden for members of the Sasquatch tribe to be out of their caves during the daylight hours, so long as they stayed within the canyon, it was far from encouraged, and it was very rare for any of her people to do so. The chances of being sighted after dawn where far greater than at night and no one wanted to take a chance of being found guilty of being sighted by outsiders because of negligence on their part.

Mala's worries about her own fate were far too great for her to be overly concerned by voices however, and she decided that her mind had been playing tricks on her because of all the stress she was under, and soon she forgot about it.

She had given up on her hopes of escape and surrendered herself to her dismal fate. She wondered how the other wives of The Other saw the world. Did any thoughts at all remain in their minds or were they truly the empty, unthinking shells that they appeared to be?

Why is this happening to me? She had asked herself over and over again. *I've done nothing to deserve this.*

After mulling this question over for the umpteenth time, Mala decided that why no longer mattered. This was happening to her and she was going to have to find a way to deal with it. She remembered her mother's advise about separating her mind from her body.

If I can only teach myself to do that really well, she thought, *maybe I will only have to let him have me once.*

180

Then I can pretend I've gone insane like the others and escape the first chance I get. Just one time and it could all be over. I just have to teach myself to separate my mind from my body, think about nothing, let my mind go blank.

Mala of course knew that The Other could read thoughts. This was one of the "magic" abilities he possessed that had helped to keep the Sasquatch Indians afraid of him. This would make things even more difficult. Even after the consummation she was going to have to keep her mind blank lest he discover her plan.

This is never going to work, she thought, then she chastised herself. *It is the only chance you've got Mala, you'd better get yourself into the right frame of mind or your only chance will be gone.*

So there Mala sat on the rock floor of the cage forcing herself to think about nothing.

When voices again came to Mala's ears. the sound didn't register right away. She had been successful in inducing herself into a trance, something like self-hypnosis. As she snapped out of it she mentally applauded herself for having been able to accomplish this. Then she thought, *if it only takes voices to break me out of my spell, how will I ever manage when The Other is invading me?* With effort she ignored the voices and tried to get her mind back into the state that it had been in.

Then a realization struck her. Those weren't voices from anyone in her tribe. Although muffled she was still able to distinguish that they spoke in a language different from hers. They had to belong to outsiders and she knew these voices were coming from the gold cave.

181

But how did they get in there without getting caught? The Other always knows when outsiders are near. How had it been possible for them to get right inside our camp?

Mala who was already overwhelmed by everything that was happening to her came to a sudden conclusion. *It's a trick,* she thought. *The Other knows what I am up to and he's trying to distract me.* As paranoid as she knew this idea was, Mala believed it. *I must be on to something with this plan,* she thought, *otherwise he wouldn't be interfering.* She drifted back into her trance.

36.

With Shawn in the lead and Lester bringing up the rear, the boys slowly and carefully made their way into the tunnel. They were all being careful to let themselves brush up against the ceiling as little as possible. Some spots were a tight squeeze however, and in these places more dust and dirt fell from above. They also found that they had to place each step softly. Too much vibration also caused dirt and dust to fall. They were already dirty and knew that by the time they got out of there they would be filthy.

"I can't see a fucking thing," said Carl rather loudly, and he immediately discovered that it was best to talk as little as possible when a large clump of rocky dirt landed on his head.

"Shhh!" Hissed someone from behind him.

Ever so slowly they continued on their way. Often times they had to crawl on their hands and knees when the tunnel became too low to walk in even if they crouched down. By the time they had reached a spot where the ceiling rose and looked as if it were going to continue to rise for a stretch, Shawn had already found four additional nuggets. His heart was pounding with excitement. Indeed it certainly was looking like Jake's gold mine hadn't merely been a myth after all.

They reached a section where the ceiling was easily fifteen feet high. Here, Shawn and Lester carefully played their flashlight beams along the floor. They found two more nuggets, the second of which could hardly be called a nugget, for it was larger than a softball.

"Wow!" Said Carl. "Look at the size of that thing. I wonder how much it's worth?"

183

"I don't know," answered Shawn who was holding onto it, "but it's got to be worth a lot."

All of the boys began a loud, animated conversation and forgot about how close to caving in the tunnel seemed to be. Denny had taken the flashlight from his brother and had wandered a little further on his own. Where he now was, the ceiling and width of the tunnel had decreased dramatically, but beyond a circular hole, he could see that it got wider again. He peered through this hole and gasped in disbelief.

"Hey you guys! Come and take a look at this!" He yelled, and then he stepped through the opening. The other five boys soon followed.

They stood side by side in a row in a huge cavern with their mouths agape. They saw gold in every direction they looked. It appeared that the walls and ceiling of this cavern were made up more of gold than rock. It was embedded into a floor which was littered with nuggets that had fallen from the walls and ceiling.

"Someone please tell me that I'm not just dreaming," said Carl.

"You're not," said Bobby. "This is all gold, and we are the richest fuckers in the world."

"Woo hoo!" Bellowed Denny, and the others joined in, their voices echoing loudly throughout the cavern and the unstable tunnel they had just gone through to get here. As their whooping reached it's loudest point, a rumbling sound could be heard coming from somewhere along the tunnel.

"What's that?" Asked Bobby.

"Thunder?" Said Carl.

Then a thick cloud of dust came pouring through the small entrance to the cavern.

184

"A cave in," said Denny.

The boys ran to the far wall of the cavern, away from the intruding dust. The rumbling sound stopped, it hadn't lasted long, but they all felt that there was a good chance that they were in serious trouble.

"I wonder how bad it is," said Shawn.

"There's only one way to find out," replied Bobby.

"I wonder how much time we have," said Carl.

"How much time for what?" Asked Denny.

"Before we suffocate," answered Carl. "Haven't you ever heard about miners getting trapped? If they're not killed by falling rocks and shit falling on them in a cave-in they suffocate before anyone can dig them out."

"We're not going to suffocate butt wipe," said Bobby.

"How do you know?"

"There's lots of air in here, this cavern is huge."

"But what if we can't get out? No one even knows we're here. If we can't dig ourselves out we'll eventually run out of air."

"Well ain't you just Mr. Positive Thinker," said Bobby. "We don't even know how bad it is and you're already worried about suffocating. If we all had your attitude we would die for sure."

"Well it happens," said Carl.

Bobby rolled his eyes, then he began picking some of the gold nuggets up off of the floor and stuffing them into his pockets.

"What are you doing?" Asked Carl.

"What does it look like I'm doing you knot head? You should be doing the same thing. When we get out of here we're going to have to figure out how to get all of this gold out of here without having to climb up and down the wall, but for this trip we'll have to do it this way."

Carl looked at Bobby dumbly, but already he saw that Shawn and Denny were loading their pockets as well. He shrugged and began picking up gold.

It wasn't until after Bobby, Carl, and the Jackson brothers had loaded themselves up with as much as they could carry that they thought about Lester and Johnny, they were no where to be seen. The others had been so focused on the gold that they hadn't even noticed their absence. Not that they were ever overly talkative, the twins had been pretty quiet ever since they had entered the tunnel. Shawn and Denny now had the two flashlights and they played the beams around the cavern, finally finding the twins sitting face to face in one of their trances in front of the small, rounded entrance to the cavern. This was now a familiar site to the others so they didn't bother saying anything. Instead they waited until they were finished.

"What's going on now?" Asked Bobby.

"He was scanning again," said Lester.

"Where is he now?" Asked Denny.

"Outside of the canyon," answered Johnny. "He's been looking for us."

"So he knows we're here?"

Lester shook his platinum head, a head that was now covered with dirt. *So they can get dirty,* thought Denny. He had been beginning to think that the two were somehow immune to it. Johnny looked over at him and smiled, and Denny was certain that this last thought had just been read.

"He's confused," said Lester. "He's still not one hundred per cent sure that we're here, or how many of us there are. Not knowing bothers him."

186

"As far as we can tell, he thinks that there is only one of us," continued Johnny. "We've been able to block him every time he's tried scanning since that first time we felt him trying to read Denny."

"We've also been able to read a lot of his thoughts over the last little while," said Lester, "and since he's not really of this dimension we shouldn't be able to."

"We think that we've been able to read him only because he's somewhat distraught over his inability to find us," added Johnny. "He's also been living with people for a long time and he's become a little more reliant on earthly laws and humans than he likes to be."

"How many people has he been living with?" Asked Shawn.

"Lots," said Johnny. "It's a tribe of Indians."

"Sasquatch?" Asked Carl.

Lester and Johnny both nodded. "They're the ones," said Lester. The same ones that creepy old lady in the museum told us about."

"Are they really cannibals?" Asked Carl.

"Yes," answered Johnny.

"How far away from us are they?" Asked Denny.

"Not very far at all," said Lester. "In fact, I think we're almost right on top of them."

Carl whistled through his teeth.

"We'd better be more careful when we get out of here," said Bobby. "Everyone make sure they talk in whispers from now on, and even then, only when we really have to."

The boys began to make their way out of the cavern and back into the tunnel.

37

Mala had been once again snapped out of her trance by a rumble. The mine was next to the cave that she was being held in, and was separated only by a rock wall maybe two feet thick. Part of this wall had fallen into the tunnel and a thick cloud of dust poured towards her making her nose burn. She was thrown into a coughing fit until the dust settled.

Mala knew that eventually the men of her tribe would clean the rubble out. It wasn't the first time there had been a cave-in in the tunnel, and she was sure that it wouldn't be the last. It looked like once the way had been cleared this time though there would be a new entrance through this cave too. When the dust settled, Mala could make out the outline of the tunnel in spite of the rock and dirt that had filled it.

All of the Sasquatch wore jewelry made out of gold from this mine. They had no understanding of money or that gold could be cashed in for it, all they knew was that it was pretty and was easy to fashion into bracelets and pendants and such. The Other had warned them of the dangers of this gold being discovered.

"They are strange these outsiders," he had said. "Gold sends them into a frenzy. You must always be careful not to leave any of it where they might happen upon it. If one outsider should find gold here, this whole canyon would soon be swarming with them. If that were to happen, it wouldn't take them long to find all of us, and then they would kill us, every last one of us."

It was warnings such as these that had made the Sasquatch Indians so deathly afraid of outsiders.

Everything they had heard about them was bad. As a result, they firmly believed that everyone outside of their tribe was evil, thus firming their resolve never to be discovered.

As Mala looked at the rubble she again questioned the origin of the voices she had heard earlier. *Maybe someone really has managed to get in after all.*

38

When the boys made it to the pile of rubble that had been left from the cave-in they noticed that already one of the flashlights was beginning to dim. They didn't like the idea of being trapped without any light.

"We'd better turn one of them off for now," said Bobby, "and then when the batteries for one die we'll still have the other."

Shawn was carrying the brighter of the two flashlights and he turned it off.

"It's going to take forever to move all of that shit out of the way," said Carl. "We're never going to get out of here."

"Fuck Carl," said Bobby. "You're such a fucking inspiration for us all."

"Well just look at it!" Said Carl, his voice on the edge of hysteria. "We're fucked."

"No Carl, we're not fucked, you are," said Bobby. "Yes, we're in a tight spot, but what do you want to hear? Want me to say that we all might just as well lie down right now and die? Is that what you think we should do? If we all sit around and whine the way you always are that's exactly what's going to happen. We'll die."

All of the boys were paying close attention to this conversation and waited to hear what Carl was going to say next, but he didn't say anything, he just looked back at Bobby whom they all knew Carl idolized, looking thoroughly ashamed of himself as tears streamed down his face. It was an awkward moment.

Bobby winked at Carl. "Don't worry bud," he said. "We'll get out of here. Do you guys see what I see?"

"What's that?" Asked Shawn dryly.

"Most of this is small rocks and dirt. It's all loose, it won't be to hard to dig."

The others saw that Bobby was right. Denny scooped up a handful to test it.

"For all we know only a small section has caved in," Bobby continued, "but even if all of the tunnel from here to the exit is plugged it's not that far, we can still get out with a little bit of elbow grease."

The rest of the boys decided that it was best to believe him. Bobby walked a distance away from the pile of rubble and emptied the gold from his pockets. "I don't want to dig lugging all of this shit around," he said, and the others emptied their pockets as well.

39

The debris from the cave-in did turn out to be fairly easy to dig just as Bobby had said. The boys were clearing the tunnel that was just enough for them to be able to squeeze themselves through, but even still their progress was slow. They had formed themselves into a line and took turns at the lead where they would dig at the rock and dirt and push it behind themselves, then the next person in line would push it back further and so on until it was all the way back to the beginning of the cave-in. If they had to dig all the way out to the canyon wall it was going to take them until sometime the following day to free themselves, but at least now they were all confident that eventually they would get out.

As the hours wore on, the boys did have a couple of concerns, they were low on water, and the second flashlight was beginning to dim, the batteries for the first had already gone dead, and they knew they didn't have much longer before they would be digging in total darkness.

"When the light goes out," said Bobby, "we can't panic. It's going to make things a lot harder, but we'll still be able to feel our way around. In the meantime, we'd better dig as fast as we can."

The boys increased their efforts and began making more impressive progress.

Shortly after Denny took his turn at the lead he noticed a small hole to his left. He was sure that he could see faint light through this hole. He was just about to call back to the others to report his discovery when all the rock and dirt on his left side fell away, he went with it.

Denny landed hard. A rock that had tumbled out of the tunnel with him ended up under him and for a moment Denny was sure that he had broken some ribs. When the pain in his side ebbed to a dull ache, Denny suddenly sensed a presence near by. He was sure that someone was watching him and he felt the small hairs on the back of his neck stand on end. In spite of the fall he had managed to hold onto the flashlight. Although it was now only casting a dull glow, he held the flashlight up and slowly shone it around him noticing as he did so that some light was seeping into the cave he had fallen into from outside. He knew that it was getting late and he was sure that this light had to be close to the last the sun would be sharing for this day. Then he saw the cage and the girl inside.

Immediately Denny recognized her. There was no mistaking her beautiful face or those big, liquid-brown eyes. She was the girl he had seen hiding in the tall grass during the scout hike. He was reminded of the uncanny resemblance she bore with Nicole, and of course, Candace. With the exception of her copper-toned skin, she could have easily passed for their sister, the third of triplets.

She's in a cage, Denny thought as he looked at her. *Why is she in a cage?*

"Are you all right?" Denny heard a voice call from the tunnel. Bobby had been behind Denny while they had been digging and had seen what had happened.

Hearing Bobby's loud voice Denny saw Mala's eyes grow larger still and an expression of panic crossed her face. She turned towards what obviously was the opening to the cave where the dying light of day was filtering in and then she turned back towards Denny with a finger over her lips, the gesture was unmistakable.

193

Denny stood so his head was now level with the hole in the wall he had fallen out of. With the flickering glow of the flashlight he could see Bobby's concerned face.

"Yes," he whispered. "I'm okay, but we've got to be really quiet."

Denny aimed the flashlight towards Mala.

"Wow," whispered Bobby. "What's she doing in there?" He whispered back to the other boys behind him. "No one say a word. Follow me as quietly as you can."

When all of the boys were in the cave standing beside Denny, they couldn't help themselves from gaping at the beautiful girl in the cage who wore nothing but a small loin cloth.

"Let's get her out of there," whispered Denny. "Give me your knife Carl."

Carl fumbled through his pockets before finding the Swiss army knife he had brought with him and handed it over to Denny. "What if she freaks out and brings the rest of them in here?" He asked as soon as the knife was in Denny's hands.

"She won't," said Lester.

"How do you know?"

"Because she wants to get out of this canyon even more than we do. She's the one who has to marry the other mind reader and she doesn't want to," said Johnny.

"She can help us get out of here faster too," said Lester. "She knows the area a lot better than we do and we don't have much time left. The rest of her people will be up soon if they aren't already. They are all going to gather just outside of this cave for the wedding. If we don't get out of here now, we're never going to see the outside of this canyon again."

No one needed the Sabina twins to elaborate any further, and they went to work on freeing Mala.

Whatever it was that had been used to bind the pieces of the cage together proved to be hard to cut even with a knife. Denny sawed away at what looked to be some sort of vine that had been hardened probably with sap of some kind. Sensing ever increasing urgency through Mala to complete the task at hand, Denny worked frantically. When he had a joint close to being severed, him, Bobby, and the others tugged away at it as hard as they could until the vine relented and then Denny continued on to the next joint until Mala was finally free. The now uncaged girl looked at the boys, specifically Denny, with unmistakable gratitude, then she again held her finger to her lips signaling silence, and led them towards the opening of the cave.

40

As they peered out of the hole in the canyon wall, the boys could see that the entrance to the cave was camouflaged by shrubs just as the entrance to the mine had been. They could also see that the sun was very low to the horizon. They knew that they didn't have much time left. Mala grabbed Denny by the arm and led him outside, the others began to follow until they saw that Lester and Johnny were again in one of their trances.

"C'mon you guys," hissed Bobby in a low voice. "We don't have time for any of that shit."

The twins remained in the mouth of the cave, sitting face to face unfazed by what Bobby had just said.

"C'mon you two," pleaded Bobby again. "Do you want to get eaten?"

The Sabina brothers stayed motionless for a while longer before snapping out of their spell and acknowledging Bobby.

"Finally," said the prospective football player.

"He's on his way back," whispered Lester.

"He's very close now. We think he was just scanning one more time before giving up on his search outside of the canyon."

"All the more reason for us to hurry the fuck up," said Bobby.

Mala was also growing impatient and was pulling hard on Denny's arm. He had stopped moving to listen in on the quiet conversation when a thought came to him. "Can you tell where he is?" He asked the twins. "What if he's coming down the wall in the same spot while we're going up?"

No one had thought about this, but with Mala now almost yanking Denny's arm out of it's socket, they knew that they didn't have much of a choice. They were just going to have to take their chances.

Denny was amazed by Mala's speed. He knew that if she were to let go of his arm she cold easily outrun all of them. It was plain to see how frightened she was of getting caught. Denny didn't know for sure what it was that she was so afraid of, but he assumed that it must have been this other mind reader that Lester and Johnny had been talking about. He found himself terrified of being caught by him as well even though he had never even seen him.

They had been running north, back into the direction of where the boys had entered the canyon from. When they reached the series of ledges where they had made their descent, Mala stopped and waited for the rest of the boys to catch up with her and Denny. When Carl, who had been bringing up the rear as usual, assembled with the rest of them, he was huffing and puffing badly. His friends knew that he wasn't in very good physical shape to begin with. He spent too much time if front of the television playing video games and eating snack cakes. All of this physical exertion over the last few hours had really taken a toll on him. His face was a pasty white color and he looked like he was just about ready to keel over at any minute. When Denny and the others looked at him they were a little worried.

"Are you OK Carl?" Asked Shawn.

"Yeah," wheezed Carl. "I'm fine," he was making a wheezing sound as he gasped for breath. "Why wouldn't I be?"

"Just checking," replied Shawn.

"Fatty here is all right," said Bobby. "You're just getting your second wind aren't you Carl?"

"Ass hole," said Carl.

"See? Told you," said Bobby.

Mala didn't understand a single word of what the boys were saying, nor did she care much what they were talking about at present. Her only concern was to get as far away from the canyon as possible as quickly as possible. This was her only chance to escape having to marry The Other and she wasn't about to let it go to waste." She began running up the series of ledges, Denny and the others quit talking and followed. It would have been impossible for them to have kept up with her had she not stopped periodically to let them catch up.

They had just begun to climb the more difficult portion of the canyon wall past the big ledge where Lester and Johnny had found that first gold nugget when they heard an incredibly loud wail coming from the direction of the mine.

"What the fuck is was that?" Asked Bobby.

"That was him, the other mind reader," said Lester. "He knows that the girl has escaped."

"He knows where we are," said Johnny. "Her tribe is going to come after us now," he nodded towards Mala.

Mala hastened her pace and quickly left the boys far behind. She looked at them with a pleading urgency in her eyes.

"OK, we'd better hurry the fuck up," said Bobby. "Let's get to camp and get on the ATVs."

They could now hear a loud commotion coming from where they had escaped, the Indians were organizing themselves. The boys climbed as quickly as they could, but daylight was fading fast and it was getting harder and

198

harder for them to be able to see where they were putting their hands and feet as they clung precariously high up on the canyon wall. A mistake from here would be fatal, there was no question about it.

Bobby could hear Carl gasping for breath from behind him.

"Not gonna make it," said Carl.

Then Mala and the boys could hear the war whoops of the Sasquatch Indians. Bobby looked into the direction of the sound. The canyon floor was now almost completely shrouded in darkness, but just enough light remained for him to be able to make out the faint shapes of their pursuers. There was only a small group of them in the lead, but not too distantly following them was a larger group, much larger, more than a hundred. Bobby couldn't tell for sure, but perhaps two or even three hundred.

"You're going to make it," Bobby hollered down to Carl, "but you're going to have to give it everything you've got. If those fuckers down there catch you they're going to roast you alive.

Bobby turned his attention back to the wall and he could hear Carl laboring for air just below him, but at least he was again moving upward.

Mala had made it to the top. She reached down to help Denny up, and soon afterwards Shawn, Lester, and Johnny stood at the lip of the canyon with them.

"C'mon ya fat fucker," they could hear Bobby say. "We're almost there, hurry the fuck up."

Under ordinary circumstances this would have struck Denny and Shawn as funny, but they could also hear the Indians. The Sasquatch were now on the canyon wall somewhere below Bobby and Carl. Denny knew how much easier the climb had been for Mala than it had been

199

for them and he knew that it would be the same for the rest of the Sasquatch. They were quickly running out of time if they hadn't already.

Finally Bobby's hand grasped the seemingly solid ground on the lip of the canyon. Denny reached down to take the hand so he could help his friend the rest of the way up, but just before he could touch it the earth beneath it crumbled and Bobby's hand slipped away. Bobby's panicked cry could be heard as he began to reel backward. Denny was sure that the big red head was doomed to fall to his death, but then a loud grunt could be heard coming out of Carl.

"Ya trying to kill me ya clumsy bastard," yelled Carl as Bobby fell into him. Then showing more strength than any of them had known he possessed including Carl himself, he managed to get a free hand on Bobby's back before his feet could break loose from the tiny ledge he was standing on. Carl pushed Bobby back tight against the wall where he could grab a new hand hold. Bobby quickly grabbed the lip again and this time pulled himself up to the top with the help of those who had already made it to safety.

Denny and Shawn laid on their stomachs and peered down into the canyon. They reached for Carl who was now only a couple of feet out of reach. They could see the Sasquatch Indians below Carl and judged that at best they might now only have a five minute lead on them. Carl looked downwards as well to see where they were, this was a big mistake for someone who was as afraid as heights as he was. He spun back towards the wall and pressed his body tight to it, he clung there frozen with fear.

"Hurry Carl," said Denny. "They're almost here."

Carl glanced up at Denny and Shawn and their outstretched hands, his eyes huge with fear. Unexpectedly he lurched upwards for them, but missed by a foot.

"Shit!" Cried Denny.

The lurch had left Carl completely off balance and he was unable to regain a hold on the wall as he leaned away from it awkwardly. He still had his gaze locked on Shawn and Denny, but now there was nothing but absolute terror in his eyes.

"Grab the wall!" Yelled Shawn, but Carl, with his free arm now pin wheeling wildly in the air was unable to. His awkward center of gravity inched him farther away from the rock wall until his foot slipped from the ledge that it had been planted on, and both Denny and Shawn could see the sheer horror on their friends face as he began to fall. It was a sight they would never forget, and one they would see over and over again in their dreams for a long time to come. They wouldn't forget his screams either. Their friend's terrified wail as he plunged to his death was probably the worst thing all of them would remember about this whole ordeal. In days to come, the surviving members of the group would also think that Carl's death had most likely saved their lives because during his plummet he hit four of the Sasquatch Indians who were leading the pursuit causing them to fall to their deaths as well and delaying the rest of the hunters for a moment to buy Mala and the boys precious seconds.

There was a silence when Carl's scream stopped. They all felt sickened. The silence was broken by Denny. "Run," he said.

"What if he's alive?" Asked Bobby. "We can't just leave him here."

"He's dead," said Lester.

201

"How do you know? You can't know that for sure."

"You know how far of a drop that was," said Shawn. "There's nothing we can do for him now."

Bobby was visibly shaken. Carl would have been surprised to know just how badly his death had affected his idol. In life he'd had no idea of just how greatly Bobby had valued their friendship.

Unsure of what Bobby was going to do, Denny repeated himself, "run!" Then he grabbed Mala's arm and it was his turn to lead her. The rest of the little group followed including Bobby. None of them knew how much of a lead they still had on the Sasquatch Indians and they half expected to feel a spear or arrow pierce their backs at any moment. All they had to do was make it the short distance to the ATVs and get them moving, then they would make it to safety, but right now that short distance sure seemed like a long ways away.

When the little red quads were in his sight, Denny saw movement from the corner of his eye. They had just gone by the path where he had first seen Mala hiding in the tall grass. As Denny ran for all he was worth he dared to look towards the movement in the heavily shadowed field beside them. Running across this field at an inhuman speed was a short, powerfully built, black man with a tiny head and a wild mass of hair. This guy was going to catch them before they got to the ATVs no matter what they did.

No! Thought Denny, and he forced himself to look away. He knew that running was the only thing left for them to do and he focused again on the ATVs. Everything seemed to be moving in slow motion to him as he waited to feel the little man's claws dig into his back. Still he ran, his lungs burned and his legs felt like rubber, but still he ran.

He was amazed when they reached the quads. He had been certain that Mr. Hair Do was going to stop them.

Mala seemed confused when Denny let her arm go and mounted one of the ATVs. Denny patted the seat behind him to try and get her to understand that he wanted her to get on, he also took this opportunity to take a quick look around to see what had happened to the strange little man. When he saw nothing he didn't know what to make of it, but at present there wasn't enough time for him to dwell on it. Shawn, Lester, and Johnny had caught up with Denny and Mala. When they quickly piled onto the second ATV Mala suddenly understood what it was that Denny had wanted her to do, and she climbed onto the seat behind Denny. When Shawn brought his little machine to life, Denny could feel Mala jump at the loud noise it produced, but she stayed put. Soon Bobby was sitting behind Mala, he was still stuck in the moment of when Carl had fallen, but at least he now seemed to realize that there was no hope that his friend had survived the fall.

Denny started his quad and then looked over his shoulder. In the last light of day he could see that three of the Sasquatch Indians had finished their climb and were running flat out towards them. Denny twisted his right hand down on the throttle and they were off. He knew that as fast as the Sasquatch were, they wouldn't be able to keep up with them now. He wasn't quite sure about the hair do guy however. The mere sight of the little man running like that had scared the hell out of him.

The first quarter mile of their journey home was smooth sailing, a natural clearing allowed the boys to run their little quads at full speed without them having to worry about running into anything and they quickly put distance between themselves and the Indians. After that they had to

203

slow down for a short ways as they maneuvered through a small section of rocks and trees, and then they were onto another straight-away. As they sped along this other long, unobstructed section, Denny was confident that they had gotten away from the Sasquatch. Up to now he had been so focused on their flight that he hadn't noticed that Mala had wrapped her arms around his neck as she clung to him from behind. The chase and the noise of the quads had frightened her so badly that she was all but strangling him without her realizing it. Gently, Denny took one of her hands and eased it from his throat to his waist. She put her remaining hand there on her own.

They were nearing a small gully where they would again have to slow down for a time when Denny saw something that made him think he was having hallucinations. The little man with the wild hair was racing from a line of trees ahead of them and to their right, he was running directly into their path.

He couldn't possibly have already run this far that fast, he thought. *It just isn't possible. Doesn't he get tired?*

Denny and Shawn slowed their machines down.

"You see that?" Yelled Shawn over the sound of the engines.

Denny nodded.

"What'll we do?"

Think fast, think fast, Denny told himself. He thought about what was behind them. *As long as we keep moving the Indians won't catch us.* Then he made a decision.

"Go!" He said. "If that fucker gets in the way run him over."

Denny clenched his teeth and twisted the throttle as far as it would go, his brother did the same and they raced towards The Other. As they sped closer and closer Denny began to believe that they really were going to have to mow the little man down. He showed no signs that he had any intention to move out of their way. Denny readied himself for the inevitable collision. It was going to be him and not Shawn who was going to run him over. He wondered what the result of the impact was going to be. Would the weight of the ATV, him, and his passengers allow them to run like a steamroller over the wild man, or would they all be thrown ass over teakettle off of the quad? He decided that it was better not to think about it.

I hope I kill you, you son of a bitch! He thought, and then he closed his eyes.

Sure that he was going to feel a thud at any moment, Denny waited a few seconds, but when nothing happened he opened his eyes again. The man was gone and they were almost into the gully. Denny hit both the hand and foot brakes, if they flew into the gully at this speed, it would probably result in one or all of them breaking their neck. Just as he thought he had been too late to avoid catastrophe, the quad slowed enough for him to be able to maneuver the little machine through the gully without spilling himself or either of his two passengers. Luckily there were no boulders or logs lying in wait for them either. He could still hear Shawn's ATV close behind them, and he knew that they had made it as well.

41

Luckily the ATVs were equipped with headlights. Otherwise it would have been impossible for Mala and the boys to have made it back to the loop and Bobby's truck that night. None of them would have felt very comfortable if they'd had to camp out for the night.

The whole way back Denny kept an eye out for the little man whom he knew without asking was the other mind reader. He was certain that Mr. Hair Do would make another appearance before the night was over, but their luck held and there was no further sign of him. No one had mentioned the wild man again during their trip back, they hadn't really talked about anything at all, they were too intent on getting home as quickly as possible.

When Bobby's truck finally came into view the boys were all overwhelmingly relieved.
When their flight from the canyon had begun, none of them had really believed that they would ever see their homes again. They had also expected that when they made it to the loop they would find that the truck was either missing or had been destroyed. They wouldn't have been at all surprised if they had found a band of Sasquatch Indians waiting there for them either, but none of that happened.

They pulled up to the dilapidated old pickup and were now so confident that they had indeed gotten away that they even took the time to load the ATVs into the truck's box. Once they had all squashed themselves into the cab and were safely moving down the road, they finally had the chance to talk.

"We should probably go straight to the police station," said Shawn.

"No one's going to be there now," said Denny.

"By the time we get there it'll be six, someone will be there by then."

"Six?" Denny had lost track of time, but still he thought that six would be too early for there to be anyone at the Vollmer's Hollow Police Station. "Constable McClean won't be out of bed at six. He probably doesn't get up until noon."

Shawn chuckled a little at this. He didn't really believe that Constable McClean slept that late, but if he did it probably wouldn't have mattered. The Hollow was hardly the crime capitol of the world. Other than having to lock up the occasional drunk in the town's single celled jail he didn't know if their chief of police had to do anything at all.

"Let's talk to your dad," said Bobby. "He'll know what to do."

This had been the first thing that Bobby had said since Carl's death. It looked like he was beginning to get control of himself again.

"Good idea," said Denny. Him and Shawn both knew that they had been pretty lucky in the father department. *Even still,* thought Denny, *Dad's going to have a hard time believing the story we've got to tell him.* Mala was still with them however, and that would lend a little more credibility to their tale.

Now that the danger was behind them, Denny was becoming very aware of Mala. It would have been impossible for him not to, she was still wearing nothing but a loin cloth and she was sitting on his lap with her head on his shoulder.

"Can you two tell what she's thinking about now?" Denny asked the twins.

"A little," said Lester. "It's hard though because a lot of what she is thinking is in words."

"She's worried about her mother," said Johnny. "She's afraid that her mother might be punished by that witch doctor because of her escape."

"Witch doctor?" Said Shawn.

Johnny shrugged, "what else could you call him?"

"What are we going to do with her?" Denny said, he nodded at Mala, but was talking more to himself than to anyone else.

"She sure does look like Nicole doesn't she," said Shawn.

Denny nodded. He had been trying not to think about Nicole, but now he found himself thinking that if she were to find herself a new boyfriend in Seattle, he hoped that she would be happy, and that the new guy knew how lucky he was. Denny was accepting the fact that it was probably a pretty unreasonable expectation on his part for her to wait for the day when he would be able to move to Seattle as well, a day that in reality, was probably never going to come.

A new day was beginning to dawn when they made it to the quiet, maple-lined streets of Vollmer's Hollow. They went to the Jackson's house and Shawn and Denny went inside while the others stayed in the truck. Twenty minutes later a bed-headed Mike Jackson came out without his sons.

"Why don't all of you come on inside," he said. "I just put on some coffee. You can all tell me what happened, and later we'll go and see Constable McClean."

Bobby opened his door and stepped out, but Mala was sitting closest to the passenger door and of course hadn't understood a word that Mike had said. Shawn and

Denny had only had time to mention her briefly and they had omitted the fact that she was all but naked. Mike was immediately stricken by her beauty.

"That must be the girl from the canyon," he said to Bobby.

Bobby nodded.

"She sure is a looker."

Mala was looking openly at Mike while doing nothing to hide her bare breasts.

"You guys could have given her a shirt," said Mike. "She doesn't seem to care much though does she?" Then he went around to her door to let her out. Now that he was near her he saw that the Indian girl was afraid of him.

"Don't worry young lady, there's nothing to be afraid of any more," he said. He held the door wide with one hand and gestured with the other for her to come out.

Mala stepped out of the truck cautiously, but she still appeared to be quite nervous.

"See," said Mike in a soothing voice, "everything is going to be okay."

Lester followed Mala out of the truck, and Johnny was just about to when she bolted. Like a flash she was out on the road before anyone could stop her and she had almost gotten herself run over by old man Hoover who was out tossing this mornings edition of the Tamarack News onto the lawns of the subscribers on his route. Hoover hit his horn and the loud blare of it made Mala run even faster.

"Wow, look at her go," said Mike, obviously impressed by her speed.

Bobby trotted after her for a few paces, but he could see that any efforts to catch her on foot would be futile. "Come back!" He yelled even though he knew that she wouldn't listen to him.

209

Shawn and Denny had stepped out of the house and watched Mala run down the street until she disappeared about a block away.

She's gone into the park, Denny thought. *Mine and Nicole's park, she's as good as gone now.* He knew that just behind the park there was a field, and just beyond that a forest. Once in the forest Mala would be at home.

"Why would she go and run off like that?" Asked Bobby.

"She was afraid to be here," said Lester. "She feels much more comfortable in the wilderness."

"Won't that other mind reader find her?"

Lester shrugged, "I don't know, but if he does it won't be for a while. He's got bigger things to worry about now."

"Like what?"

"Him and his people have been seen," said Johnny. "He knows that we'll tell others that they're down there."

"I thought you said you couldn't read his mind," said Bobby.

"We can't, we're just putting two and two together."

"Maybe Mala will come back," said Denny. "Do you two think she will?"

"We can't tell," said Johnny, "but I don't think so."

"Let's have our coffee out here on the lawn," said Mike. "That way if she does come back we'll be able to see her coming."

Mike, Shawn, and Denny went back into the house and returned a moment later with hot coffee for everyone. Already the day was promising to be another hot one, and they sat in the shade of a large maple growing on the Jacksons' yard. For a short while no one said anything, but once the boys got around to telling Mike about what had been happening over the last couple of days it seemed that they couldn't talk fast enough. Often two or three of them talked at the same time giving Mike a hard time in keeping up.

When the clock crept past 9:00 AM they knew that it was time to talk to Constable McClean. They also knew that Mala wasn't coming back, but they had all really known that as soon as she had fled.

42

Constable McClean had arrived at Vollmer's Hollow's little police station at a little before 8:00 AM. It was true that there was little law enforcing to be carried out in the little town, and it really wasn't necessary for him to come in so early, but his salary was coming from taxpayers and he figured that he owed it to them to at least keep up regular hours.

The police chief enjoyed his mornings. Even at the height of the business day, the Vollmer's Hollow Police Station could hardly be described as bustling with activity, but he did have two day deputies and a dispatcher/secretary to share it with. They didn't come in until 9:00 AM, so when he came in at his usual time Alex McClean had almost a whole hour entirely to himself. He spent this hour reading the Tamarack News and drinking coffee. This morning as he carried on with his daily ritual he had no idea of how far from ordinary this day was going to be.

It was shortly after his two day deputies and the dispatcher, Pamela had reported for work when Mike and the boys came into the station.

Constable McClean and Mike had been friends for years, but Constable McClean couldn't remember ever seeing Mike in the station before today. Mike looked around after entering, and when he spotted the police chief he headed towards him followed by the five boys.

"Good morning Mike," said Constable McClean. He was genuinely happy to see his friend. "What brings all of you here?"

"I'm afraid that I've got some bad news," said Mike. "These boys tell me that Carl was killed in the canyon."

"What?" Said the constable. "Carl Montgomery?"

"Yes," answered Mike.

"What happened?" Asked Constable McClean.

Mike and the boys filled him in on all of the details. When they were done they could see that Constable McClean was having a hard time believing them.

"You're telling me that there are wild Indians in the canyon?" He asked looking at Shawn and Denny.

The boys nodded.

"What do you make of all this Mike?"

"I have no reason not to believe them."

Constable McClean drummed his fingers on his desk.

43.

The Other had enjoyed his time in the canyon, and he had hoped to remain there for many years to come, but that was no longer possible. He and the people he had chosen to hide away here with had been seen. An outsider had died here today in the presence of others, and it wouldn't be long before more of them came, this time there would be many of them and they would be angry.

The Other found the outsider's self righteous anger to be humorous. In their world they killed, raped, and performed a vast variety of other despicable acts upon their own kind each and every day, but this was something that they had grown accustomed to, something they had always lived with and known. An outsider killing an outsider had grown so common that it hardly caused a stir any longer. This was the way of life they had always known, and in some cases murder was even accepted, but The Other knew that when faced with an element of the unknown, when one of their own kind was killed by someone or something they didn't understand, they would be quick to band together in search of retribution.

The Other knew that he couldn't bring all of the Sasquatch Indians out of the canyon, when the outsiders arrived there would be a massacre, and he wanted them to believe that the entire tribe had been annihilated. He would bring only the chief, a few braves, and a few fertile women with him. Then they would have to find another place to hide and begin to rebuild a new life.

44.

Trusting in Mike's judgment of the tale the boys had just told him, Constable McClean carefully thought about what he should do. If indeed there was an entire tribe of wild Indians living in the canyon, and he was going to have to treat the situation based on that assumption, then he knew that he didn't have nearly enough manpower to deal with the situation.

"You realize that we are going to have to call in the National Guard to take care of this don't you?" Alex said to Mike and the boys.

None of them had thought about this and Mike turned to the boys and asked them one more time, "you guys aren't making all of this up are you?"

"I wish we were," answered Denny.

Mike nodded to Constable McClean with an earnest expression indicating that he believed them.

"Very well," said Alex, and he picked up the phone.

45

Mala herself didn't know why it was that she had fled. She had felt safe with the young men who had rescued her, and she had a strong attraction to the one the others had called Denny.

So much had happened so quickly, and when Mala had been taken to where the outsiders lived she had found it all overwhelming. Everything about them was so different from the life she had known in the canyon. When the boys spoke she couldn't understand them, and their dwellings seemed so elaborate.

Why would anyone live in such a big place? She wondered.

The Sasquatch Indians had stayed in their caves only to sleep unless they were sick, or when weather conditions were so harsh that they needed to take shelter. They spent the rest of their time outside and the idea that anyone would want to be in doors when they didn't have to be would have never crossed Mala's mind.

The young Indian woman had found the ride in the boys traveling machine exciting. Never would she have imagined that it would be possible to move so fast. She had heard that The Other could run faster than any man alive, but she knew that it would have been impossible even for him to have kept up with that machine.

Mala was sure that there were plenty more wonders for her to marvel at about the outsider's world, and she had to admit that a chance for her to discover all of these new things caused her great excitement, but in the end it had all been too much for her to handle all at once. She had picked a site for a temporary camp, and had begun going

216

about the business of collecting ever green boughs that she would use to make herself a shelter with. The site she had chosen wasn't far from where the outsiders lived, thus here she felt protected from The Other. From here she could try to sort everything out that was going through her mind. She was certain that she could find Denny's home again if and when she decided to return to the outsiders' world.

Mala could survive out here in the forest, but here she would have to live in solitude, and that prospect wasn't very appealing to her.

46.

After slamming the phone back into it's cradle, Constable McClean sat back in his chair at the desk and closed his eyes to try and collect himself.

It hadn't been half an hour since he had called the National Guard when the call from Raymond Stone came. After three years had passed by, Alex had forgotten all about him and the missing Eric Abel.

"I thought you were going to keep me informed about any developments in this case!" Raymond had bellowed.

That was all it had taken to jar the memory of the Vollmer's Hollow police chief. He had never met Mr. Stone, but he couldn't erase the mental image he had of him. He pictured Raymond as a little man with soft, delicate hands, and a big mouth. He didn't know where that image had come from, but that was the picture he had developed in his mind from the first telephone conversation he'd had with the man.

"We don't know that there have been any developments in the case," answered Alex.

"Well I just heard differently."

"And where did you hear that?"

"I've got a lot of connections," said Raymond. "A contact I have in the National Guard just told me quite an interesting tale about some wild Indians you've got running around up there."

Good grief, thought Constable McClean. "We're not sure yet what the situation is," he said, "and we certainly don't know if there is any connection between what you've heard and the disappearance of Eric Able."

"Of course there's a connection! What the hell else could have happened to him?"

"Sasquatch National Park is very big and ... "

"Save it," interrupted Raymond Stone. "No matter what is going on over there it's news, and the public has a right to know about it. I'm coming up there personally with a crew to cover the story."

"That might not be such a good idea," said Constable McClean. "It could be dangerous and I don't think civilians ought to be ... "

Again Raymond interrupted, "tell it to the National Guard," and then he hung up.

Alex McClean opened his eyes, the urge to break something had passed. *What an ass hole,* he thought, but he already knew that like it or not, Raymond Stone and his people from Abel-y Uncovered were going to be tagging along when the investigation in the canyon began.

The police chief took a deep breath. He also had another task that he wasn't looking forward to. He had to pay a visit to Doreen Montgomery.

47

As tired as the boys were, they weren't quite ready for sleep just yet. They were sitting in the shade of the big maple on the Jackson's front lawn, it was early, but already the day was hot. Mike had gone inside to collect a few things that he thought he might need when he led Constable McClean and the National Guard to the section of the canyon where the boys had found the Sasquatch Indians. This was the first time the boys had been able to talk amongst themselves since their return to Vollmer's Hollow.

"There's something that I don't get," said Denny

"What's that?" Asked Shawn.

"You guys all saw that little man that was chasing us right?"

"How could we miss him," said Bobby. "We almost ran right into him."

"Why didn't he stop us? I'm pretty sure that he could have if he had wanted to."

After a short hesitation Johnny spoke up. "No, I don't think he could."

"Sure he could have, he could run faster than the ATVs, he could have caught us easy." Denny paused, then added, "I know he was small, but he looked strong."

"I don't think he is capable of doing physical harm to people," said Lester. "He can only manipulate minds to make humans harm each other."

"How do you know that?" Asked Shawn.

"We don't really," answered Johnny. "It's just a feeling, but I'm pretty sure that we're right."

"I wonder what they did with Carl," said Bobby. His voice sounded distant, and the others knew that his mind was still back at the canyon wall where Carl had fallen. Denny was surprised to see a tear trickling down the big redhead's cheek.

No one knew what to say. The fact that Carl was dead hadn't fully sunk in yet, but now that the subject had been brought up, they were forced to think about him. At times Carl had possessed a rather obnoxious personality, but in spite of that, he had somehow managed to endear himself to all of them, even the Sabina twins who had only just gotten to really know him. They also thought about what Lester and Johnny had said about the Sasquatch Indians being cannibals, and it was better not to think about what they were doing with Carl's body.

The awkward silence was finally broken by Bobby. "I don't know about the rest of you guys, but I could sleep for a week. Constable McClean doesn't want us to come along when they go to the canyon, so there's not much point in keeping awake any more."

The rest of the boys agreed, and the Sabina twins accepted Bobby's offer for a ride home.

When Denny and Shawn went into the house, Shawn headed straight for bed. Mike Jackson was in the basement rooting through his camping equipment and Denny found himself alone in the living room. He thought about Nicole and decided to check for e-mail from her before going to bed. He had told her about the trip him and the others had planned, so she knew that he was going to be away for a few days, but he was sure that there would be several messages from her anyway.

After booting up the machine and connecting to the Internet however, he found only one, and he couldn't

believe his eyes as he read the message from his beloved
Nicole.

> *Dear Denny,*
> *I don't know how else to tell you this other than to
> just come right out and say it.*
> *A couple of days ago, Candace and I met another
> set of identical twins, twin brothers. We had so much in
> common that we hit it off right away, and we all want to see
> more of each other.*
> *I do love you Denny, and I will always cherish the
> time we spent together, but I can't go on forever moping
> about us not being together any more.*
> *I know that we've talked about the possibility of
> making arrangements for us to one day be together again,
> but I think that we both know that the chances of that really
> happening aren't very good.*
> *You are a wonderful guy Denny, and you will
> always have a very special place in my heart. I hope you
> find a special girl soon, and I hope she realizes how lucky
> she is to have you.*
> *love*
>
> *Nicole.*

When Denny finished reading the message he didn't
know how he felt. So much had happened over the last
couple of days that perhaps all of his emotions had been
numbed, or maybe he had been expecting just such a
message all along. He had known that this moment had
always been a possibility ever since Nicole's departure, and
Denny had thought that he had prepared himself for it.
Even still, to find that she had indeed met someone else

222

hurt, and for sure he was jealous of whoever this twin was that she had met, but a bigger part of him wanted Nicole to be happy. In his mind he saw her smiling face, and he couldn't help but smile himself at the image.

Good bye Nicole, he thought. *I hope you have a good life.* Then he bowed his head and silently cried.

48.

Raymond Stone watched from the helicopter somewhat in awe at the vast wilderness of Sasquatch National Park as they soared above it en route to Vollmer's Hollow. From the air it seemed an endless sea of trees, streams, and rock.

Raymond really didn't give a damn about Eric Abel. He never wished for any harm to come to the man, but he also never lost any sleep when Eric had gone missing either. A clause in their contract stipulated that the sole ownership of Abel-y Uncovered would be awarded to the surviving partner should either Eric Abel or Raymond Stone perish. The contract also stipulated that it would be assumed that should either partner go missing for a period of two years they would be assumed deceased. More than three years had elapsed since Eric's disappearance and Raymond Stone was now solidly recognized as the sole proprietor of Abel-y Uncovered.

Of course, when Raymond had been informed by his source in the National Guard that a tribe of Native Americans had been found hiding away in Sasquatch National Park, he immediately saw an opportunity to boost sales for the next issue of his tabloid. His feigned concern for his missing partner when he had talked to Constable McClean had only been to ensure that if indeed the story was true, he would be there to cover it.

There was a lot of competition in the tabloid industry, and although his reader's never seemed to tire of scandalous tales about their favorite celebrities, a true story about an Indian tribe untouched for centuries by time

224

would be just what he needed to pull Abel-y Uncovered ahead of the others, at least for the time period of the issue.

When Alex McClean was introduced to Raymond Stone he found that the mental image he'd had of the man had been all wrong. The man standing in front of the Vollmer's Hollow police chief was hardly the soft little man that Alex had envisioned. Constable McClean was 6'4", and Raymond was almost as tall as him. Alex judged his age to be in the mid to late fifties, and it didn't appear that he missed many meals. He had a full head of white hair, and sported a deep tan. Raymond was quick to shake Alex's hand with a firm grip, and then took over the planning for the trip to Reid's Canyon.

"Who knows exactly where the hell it is that we're going?" He asked loudly.

Slightly annoyed, Alex didn't answer.

"Well someone must know," said Raymond. "I was told that it was a group of boys who stumbled onto all of this. Where are they? Someone's going to have to get them here."

"I'm the father of two of those boys," spoke up Mike Jackson.

Alex could sense that Mike's opinion of Raymond was close to that of his own.

"Those boys have been through enough," Mike went on. "I know the spot you're looking for, and I'll take you there."

"Fair enough," said Mr. Stone. Then he looked at the captain in charge of the forty troops that had been dispatched from the National Guard and said, "the Abel-y Uncovered chopper and this man," indicating Mike, " will take the lead so we can get some clear pictures should we find anything. Your choppers will follow close behind."

225

Constable McClean waited for an objection from the captain whose name he had not been given, but none came.

What the hell is this? He wondered, *why is the National Guard taking orders from a civilian?*

Evidently Raymond Stone had some clout no matter what Alex thought of him.

49.

The helicopters from the National Guard, and the one from Abel-y Uncovered had used the football field of Vollmer's Hollow High for landing. Most of the troops had waited there while their captain and Raymond Stone had gone to pay Constable McClean a visit.

Mike and Alex were both taken aback when they had first seen these men. They were dressed in full army fatigues, and were heavily armed.

You'd think it was World War III, thought Mike, but he knew that even during field exercises these men were required to don their complete uniform and arms.

Without any further ado the men loaded themselves into the choppers. Constable McClean hopped into the one belonging to Abel-y Uncovered with Mike without bothering to wait for permission from Stone. Once the choppers were in the air, Mike gave the pilot directions, and before long they were retracing the route he and the boy scouts had taken three years earlier.

"I want you to get everything we see," Raymond ordered a man sitting in a window seat at the front of the helicopter. "Don't leave anything out."

The man he had talked to began speaking quietly into the mouthpiece of a headset he wore.

"Get some pictures of all those trees and shit down there," Raymond ordered another man. "I want the public to get a feel for how wild this place is. Let's get some video too."

Constable McClean watched silently as the Abel-y Uncovered crew went to work, all the while wondering what they were going to find when they reached their

227

destination. Then he watched the rugged landscape unfold itself beneath them.

"Okay, that's where the campsite was," Mike told the pilot when they came to it. He also noticed that none of the boys' camping equipment was there.

"Where to from here sir?" Asked the pilot.

Mike pointed towards the canyon.

As the choppers flew over the canyon's edge, Raymond Stone couldn't help but wonder why this park, Reid's Canyon in particular, didn't draw more tourists than it did. True, it wasn't as big as the far better known Grand Canyon, but it was a quite a sight to behold just the same.

Once inside the canyon, Mike saw the protrusion in the wall and knew that they were near the spot where the boys had been. Somewhere below, perhaps even directly under them, would be the spot where Carl had made impact with the ground when he had fallen.

"We can land anywhere around here," Mike instructed the pilot.

The pilot nodded, and a large, sandy patch near the river made for a perfect landing pad.

As the helicopters lowered, Mike and Constable McClean both scanned the ground near the base of the wall for signs of Carl Montgomery, but found no indication of him.

"Where to from here?" Asked Raymond Stone after the choppers had landed, and the men had collected themselves into a group.

"Let's take a closer look for that kid over there," said Alex. He pointed his finger and moved it along the bottom of the canyon wall to show where he meant.

"Very well," said Raymond, then he said something quietly into the National Guard Captain's ear, and the captain ordered his troops to begin a search for Carl.

In this section of the canyon there weren't many trees or other such obstacles to impede the men's vision, especially directly at the wall where only small patches of tall grass and weeds grew in the rocky ground. As a result their search was swift.

"This could be blood over here sir," shouted a dark-haired guardsman who didn't appear old enough to be in the service.

The captain made his way over to where the youth was standing, but not before Raymond Stone and his eager crew made it to the site where they immediately began taking pictures.

"There's more of it over there," said Raymond pointing.

Indeed there was more of a deep red substance that no one doubted was blood. The pattern that had been left on the rocks here looked to be the result of something being dragged -- or more precisely something that was bleeding very badly being dragged.

Alex felt a loathing as he caught a glimpse of Raymond Stone. The newspaper man had an unmistakable glint in his eye. It made Alex think of a vulture coming across an animal carcass.

That fucker is really enjoying this, thought the police chief. *What's he going to do if he finds a body? Drool?*

As Mike looked at the marks he couldn't help but think that it could just as easily have been Shawn or Denny's blood he was looking at now instead of Carl's. There was no doubt in his mind as to the source of the blood. Mike had liked Carl and was sad to see such a fate befall the boy who's head he had once rescued from a lawn chair, but at the moment he couldn't deny to himself that he wasn't grateful that it hadn't been one of his sons.

But where's the body?

The blood was smeared towards the protrusion on the canyon wall. Mike had listened to the boys' tale intently, and he knew that it was just beyond this protrusion where they claimed to have found the gold mine, and where they believed the Indians lived. No one had mentioned anything about the gold to either Raymond Stone or the National Guard. Both Mike and Constable McClean had decided that if the others discovered it for themselves, so be it, but they hadn't felt any need to disclose the information voluntarily.

"Where to from here?" Asked Mr. Stone.

Mike and Alex exchanged a quick glance between themselves, and then Mike pointed towards the protrusion.

50

As the men made their way, Mike Jackson, and Constable McClean walked side by side.

"Are you thinking what I'm thinking?" Asked Alex.

"About what happened to Carl's body?" Asked Mike.

The police chief nodded. There was no need for him to go into any further detail about what the Indians would have wanted the youth's corpse for.

After they had rounded the protrusion in the canyon wall, the men found the hollow section just as the boys had described to Mike and Constable McClean. They stopped for a moment to decide what to do next. Both Mike and Alex as well as quite a few of the troops from the National Guard, felt sure that they were being watched. They could hear the sound of the river a hundred yards away as it hurled itself over the rocks in the rapids, but other than that, everything was silent.

"Well, what are we waiting for?" Asked Raymond in his loud voice that seemed louder still because of the quiet around them that he was disturbing. "What should we be looking for now?"

"Caves," answered Mike.

"Caves?" Said Raymond. He walked a few paces ahead of everyone else and closely scrutinized the canyon wall as he did so. "I don't see any caves."

"The boys said that they were well hidden, they only found the one where the girl was being held prisoner."

"And you're positive that these boys of yours weren't just telling tall ... "

Shoo-whumpf!

231

Raymond Stone slowly turned around to face the rest of the men. He wore an expression of utter shock, as well that he should for he had an arrow protruding from his forehead. Then his eyes rolled back into his head, and he fell backwards. Dead.

"Everyone down!" Ordered the captain of the National Guard, and as soon as the men hit the dirt, a rain of arrows showered down upon them.

Mike could hear grunts and cries of pain as men were either struck by arrows or narrowly missed. One sank into the hard dirt only two feet from his own head. Then Mike heard wails, and as he looked up at the canyon wall he saw why it was that none of them had been able to see the caves. The openings had been camouflaged with what looked to be thin sheets of rock. Most were now opened to have allowed for that first volley of arrows, but now as Mike watched, he saw several more open, and from each new cave emerged a fiercely painted warrior.

"Holy fuck," muttered Mike, and he watched in stunned amazement as the late emergers from the caves shot arrows down at him and the other men.

"Open fire!" Ordered the captain.

An explosion of sound erupted from the troops of the National Guard as they discharged their machine guns. Mike glanced over at Constable McClean and saw that he had withdrawn his service revolver and was also shooting at the figures on the canyon wall.

The following minutes were to be forever etched into all of the men's minds. Shots erupted from exit wounds on the bodies of the Indians and splattered bloody gore on the rock wall behind them. As one body after another fell from ledges, others soon emerged from the caves to take their places, each in turn firing arrows and spears at the men on the ground below them. Eventually, as more and more of the Sasquatch Indians were shot down, the replacements on the ledges were women and children who all proved to be just as ferocious as the men had been.

Even through the sound of machine gun fire, Mike could hear the sickening pop of breaking bones, and the meaty smacks as the Indians hit the hard packed earth from their lofty perches on the wall.

Constable McClean had emptied his revolver three times during the melee'. It was the first time he had ever fired it in the line of duty, and when it was all over, he found that his face was damp with tears. He knew that some of his shots had found their mark, and he didn't like to think of how many. He detested the knowledge that he had killed other human beings, but no matter how many times he replayed the scene over in his mind in the following days, weeks, and years, he couldn't see how they could have done it any differently. They had been sitting ducks lying there on the ground like they had been. Some of the caves had been in the protrusion on the canyon wall behind them causing them to have been surrounded. It had simply been a matter of kill or be killed. Survive by any means possible, and him and the men of the National Guard, at least those who had made it, had chosen survival. When the fighting was over they found that seventeen guardsmen had been killed, and twelve more injured, making it almost three-quarters of their number to have taken at least one hit.

After the battle, reinforcements had been called in by radio, and the caves had been cautiously inspected, but all that had been found was the corpses of the Sasquatch

Indians who had been too young to have been able to join the assault. Their throats had been slit by their own people.

"It would appear that these primitive people had found death to be more desirable than capture," one newsman reported. "Even if it meant killing their own babies."

Carl Montgomery's body had been discovered in the same cave that Mala had been held captive in. He had been stripped, gutted, and hung upside down the same way a deer carcass would have been. Both Mike and Constable McClean found themselves hoping that he had indeed been dead when the Sasquatch Indians had found him.

It had also been found that the Sasquatch Indians had held a huge wealth of gold. All of them had adorned themselves with jewelry made from the precious metal. Many golden statuettes and other trinkets had also been found, but amazingly to Mike, the boys, and Constable McClean, and in spite of the numerous news teams and other visitors to the canyon following the massacre, no mention of the mine was ever made. The Jackson's, the Sabina's, and Bobby, couldn't understand why it was that with so many people in the area, none of them had discovered it. Then again, the people of Vollmer's Hollow had always liked to keep their secrets to themselves. They all knew that Jake Vollmer's gold mine was out there somewhere, but unless an outsider asked them about it directly, why mention it?

51.

The band followed their leader up to the crest of yet another hill. Judging by his expression, these remaining Sasquatch Indians knew that The Other liked what he was seeing, and they were sure that he had chosen wisely. From the hill they could see a wide stream not too far off in the distance, and the area around them appeared to be completely unmolested by the evil outsiders. This was to be their new home and with many places for them to hide, a good home it was.

The Other did a quick scan to see if he could detect any nearby, unwanted presences. Satisfied that there were none, his decision was final. He hadn't brought any of his wives, for in their dazed state they would have slowed their flight, but he knew it didn't matter, he could always take another. He thought again of Mala. He was annoyed that he didn't know where she was. If she was staying with the outsiders she would be difficult to find, but The Other felt reasonably confident that one day he would indeed see her again. After all, he had all the time in the world.

THE END